To Jean, friend, art,
my friend,
buddy, + a favorite
person. Love you
Faye Henderson

Praise for Faye Henderson

"I'm a huge fan of the Jigs Up Cozy Mystery series, and I'm an even bigger fan of one of the main characters - the super-feisty and super-sassy Ives Schnepe, PI. Ives makes becoming a PI at 62 y.o. some kind of wild and fabulous fun. This is her story, and it's a hoot! And, of course, there's a great mystery to solve, too!" --- D. D. Scott, International Bestselling Author

Sixty-two-year-old Ives Schnepe, PI, convinces her boss, Janene Ramsey - owner of the Jigs Up Agency - to take a case in Ives's small, northeastern Kentucky hometown, where a skull and a few mason jars discovered outside the entrance to a cave high up in the hills may mean a lot more is going on than a little moonshine operation. With the help of Ives' childhood best friend Rosa Leigh and Sheriff Blake Sheets, Ives' high school flame, Ives is determined to solve the case, even if it means she may not live to see it.

In this second book of the Jigs Up Cozy Mystery series, we've gone from the agency headquarters in the Florida Everglades to the hills and caves of Three Pines, Kentucky. Yes, there's a mystery to solve that is more than a little dangerous, but it's all done with a bunch of quirky-fun characters and lots of laughs among old and new friends.

Skull-Dug-gery

on

Copperhead Mountain

Jigs Up Mystery #2

Faye Henderson

First Electronic Edition: September 2019
First Print Edition: September 2019
eBook ISBN: 978-0-9991833-2-8
Print ISBN: 978-0-9991833-3-5

eBook and Print Book Design & Formatting by
D. D. Scott's LetLoveGlow Author Services

Table of Contents

Chapter 1..1
Chapter 2..7
Chapter 3..14
Chapter 4..21
Chapter 5..28
Chapter 6..37
Chapter 7..42
Chapter 8..48
Chapter 9..54
Chapter 10..58
Chapter 11..62
Chapter 12..68
Chapter 13..72
Chapter 14..81
Chapter 15..90
Chapter 16..97
Chapter 17..101
Chapter 18..106
Chapter 19..116
Chapter 20..122
Chapter 21..127
Chapter 22..132
Chapter 23..137
Chapter 24..142
Chapter 25..150
Chapter 26..159
Chapter 27..167
Chapter 28..181

Chapter 29...190
Chapter 30...195
Chapter 31...207
Acknowledgements..215
About the Author..216
Books by Faye Henderson...217

Chapter 1

Steamy vapors drifted up through the muggy air from the roadway. Traffic going into Palmetto was bumper to bumper in both lanes, which was typical in Florida, and I was in the wrong one. I turned my signal on and waited for someone to let me merge. At this point, no one would guess that we're under a hurricane watch. Business continued as usual and would do so, until we were told to evacuate. At which point, the congestion would be the same.

The vehicles finally drove forward, except the one in the next lane, so I gunned the car and filled the space. Horns blared. I don't know why they're upset. We're not going anywhere fast. At the sight of the Green Bridge, I sighed a breath of relief.

After I inched across the bridge and drove through town, I speeded up. My mission was paramount, and I didn't have time to play around in traffic. I swerved into the lane of rude speeding drivers refusing to let me in. Brakes squealed, and a gray Taurus narrowly missed running up my tail pipe. Rush hour has some stupid drivers, and the one behind me is apparently the dumbest. He laid on his horn.

"Oh, blow your nose. You'll receive more from the experience," I shouted.

He veered into the other lane and passed me.

I caught a red streak out of the corner of my eye and glanced right.

"Hey, if you want to impress me, wear a black Onyx ring on that finger. Have some respect for your elders. I'm old enough to be your mother."

He squeezed between me and the compact in front of me and slowed.

I laughed out loud.

"Okay, I deserve it," I said, as if he could hear my half-hearted apology while he sped away.

I made a quick left onto Moccasin Wallow Road.

For you who don't know me, I am Ives Schnepe, a private eye in the JIGS UP Agency in Palmetto, Florida. When Janene Ramsey, the owner of the agency, house sat for my neighbors, I met her and the other partners. I helped the ladies solve the murder of Brandy White, a woman Janene stumbled upon in a copse of trees while she was golfing. There were four of us, but Mallory Fitzpatrick, or Queenie as I called her, had recently left to care for her mother who had fallen and broken her hip. At the present time, we deal with property searches, authenticate art, perform background checks, locate missing persons and occasionally expose a cheating mate.

When I arrived at the office, Janene and Gabrielle Amstutz were hard at work.

"Good morning, Ladies! While I was off duty, I found a missing person and landed us a lucrative job," I said, scuttling to my desk, wheeling my chair between the two of them and plopping down into it. "My friend Rosa Leigh Adams sent a mysterious photo to my phone. Her grandson found a cave earlier this week when he was hiking."

I placed the phone on Janene's desk and motioned to Gabrielle. "Tell me what you see."

"A cave with an opening with trees surrounding it," Janene said, beating Gabrielle to it.

Gabrielle leaned in. "Is that a mason jar lying in the lower right corner?"

"It is," I said.

Janene lowered her head and squinted at the photo. "There are two walking sticks lying near the jar."

"And there's a tall pole with a piece of tattered rag to the left side, above the mouth of the cave," Gabrielle said, pointing to it on the screen. She eyeballed me and raised her eyebrows. "Maybe so the site can be seen from far away."

Janene leaned back in her chair. "Where is this cave?"

"In northeastern Kentucky, but don't stop looking. You've missed one important object."

Gabrielle leaned over the photo. "Twigs and leaves."

I enlarged the area at the foot of a large white oak and said, "Explore closer."

She lifted the phone and pinched the image all sorts of directions. "I don't see anything. Here, you inspect it," she said, handing the phone to Janene.

Janene studied the photo and gulped. "Is that a skull lying at the base of the tree? I can't be sure. There are saplings growing in front, blocking part of the view."

"It is," I said, slapping my leg. "Rosa Leigh wants us to find the cave and tell her, what, or who the skull belongs to."

Janene shook her head. "We don't have the finances to fly over a thousand miles to solve a mystery the local police can handle."

Raising my hands as if in surrender, although that was the last thing I was going to do, I said, "Rosa Leigh will pay the expenses, and we don't all have to go. Send me."

They looked at each other and burst out laughing.

I glowered at them. "Rosa Leigh is my friend, and I helped you with the White murder mystery, didn't I?"

Janene pulled a tissue from the box on her desk and blotted her eyes. "You helped find people who could help us investigate, but if you recall, your friend Jake did most of the leg-work...not you."

"Ives is referring to all those delicious desserts she shared with us," Gabrielle said and chuckled. "That's how she helped us."

"Desserts won't solve this mystery," Janene said, "and Jake won't be there to give us police information. We can't investigate this. We haven't a clue where to begin. We're strangers up there, with no sympathetic officer willing to help us."

I scooted forward in my chair and stared into Janene's brown eyes. "I forgot to mention I grew up in the area. Rosa Leigh and I were best friends through high school and college. I probably know the Sheriff. If I don't, Rosa Leigh will. She said you could come, Janene. I told her you're writing a book, and she offered her mother-in-law wing to you. I can investigate, and you can write."

Gabrielle picked up a pencil and tapped it against her lips. "How much is she paying?"

I placed my hands on both my legs to hold them still. "All our expenses and a hundred dollars an hour when working. She'll provide our lodging and food. Her house is huge with three bedrooms and the mother-in-law suite."

"And you know the Sheriff?" Janene asked.

I shrugged my shoulders. "I probably know him. It's a rural area and hardly anyone leaves. Me being the exception, of course."

"Why isn't the Sheriff investigating the case?" Janene asked.

"He might . . .," I rolled my eyes up, trying to think of the exact words to hook Janene, "...as soon as someone finds the skull. Rosa Leigh's grandson couldn't find the site again. When he snapped the photo, he didn't notice the skull. He was focused on the cave. When he showed the picture to Rosa Leigh, she was shocked. She didn't know there was a cave on the mountain, and when she noticed the jar, she suspected someone had a moonshine still up there and was using the cave to store supplies. She got her magnifying glass out, and that is when she spotted the skull, leaning against a tree. It was peeking through leaves."

Gabrielle arched one of her strawberry blond brows. "She's not telling us everything, Janene. The job sounds too good to be true."

I bolted from my chair so fast, it rolled to the other side of the room and banged against a file cabinet. "We won't lose money because we aren't investing any." I paced the room. "Rosa Leigh will pay for our flights, have a rental car waiting and a thousand dollars, no strings attached, just to find the cave. Solving the mystery of the skull get us extra cash."

Janene's eyes grew big. "When does she want us to start?"

"As soon as possible. She's afraid someone will stumble upon the scene."

Janene clasped her hands behind her head and leaned back. "Okay, Ives, it sounds lucrative." She gazed at

Gabrielle. "You're investigating the stolen art case. And someone needs to go with Ives. I do need time to write, and we don't dare let her go by herself. She'll be in all kinds of trouble," Janene said, winking at Gabrielle.

"I'm not deaf. Nor am I too old to have my feelings hurt. Seems to me, Janene, you were the one in peril not long ago. And why? Because you had to know who killed Brandy White. Don't look down your cute little nose. Since this house is so close to the ocean, and the storm is almost on us, you'll need to evacuate anyway. Why not keep going north?"

I saw a spark of understanding in her eyes, so I went ahead and sunk the hook. "Besides, how much trouble will I find searching for a cave and a skull in a town where I know everyone, and most people know me?"

Chapter 2

After watching the local update on the approaching hurricane, we made our places as storm-safe as possible and made haste to pack. By three o'clock that afternoon, Gabrielle, who was staying with Mallory in a no flood, no storm surge area, dropped Janene and me off at the Sarasota Airport.

To our surprise, the plane was on time. After a non-stop flight to Cincinnati, we picked up the rental car and arrived at Rosa Leigh's late evening.

As we made our way to her front door, it was almost dark. The wind swept down Copperhead Ridge Road. Cold rain pounded our skin.

I pushed the doorbell, and soft music resonated through the massive home.

We heard a shriek. Then a dog barked. Someone shushed it. A visitor at the door is no big deal in most places, but at the Adams' house in Hickory County, Kentucky, it appeared to create a panic.

I stared at Janene, wiped the blowing rain from my eyes and knocked on the door. The dog went berserk, again. A shrill voice tried to quiet it.

I placed my ear against the wet door and listened.

"Are you expecting anyone?" A male voice asked.

A female voice answered, "Not until tomorrow sometime."

After a brief pause, the male said, "Who could be out there?"

Shoes click-clacked across the floor, and the female voice said, "I don't know, but he's about to have the worst night of his life."

I prepared to wait it out until the crazies inside came to their senses, but my partner broke the silence. "Ms. Adams, it's Ives Schnepe and Janene Ramsey. I'm sorry if we scared you. Your friend Ives assured me you wouldn't mind if we came a day early," Janene said, her fierce, angry eyes burning into mine.

I stared at the metal door in front of me. I knew my place and wasn't about to scold my boss or make excuses I didn't have. Researcher, spy, interviewer – those are the best descriptions of me and my talents, and the reason some call me nosy. Oh, and I'm a baker, too. No one disputes that skill. However, I definitely may have been a bit out of my league as a decision-making employee.

The door latch clicked.

Startled, I jumped back.

"Be ready to run for your life," I warned Janene, who looked at me with a mix of horror and the rage that was now about to get the best of her.

The door jerked open with such force I felt the pull. A 9mm gun was fixed between my eyes.

Everything went black. My legs wobbled. I thought I was going to pass out.

Rosa Leigh finally lowered the weapon. "Oh, good lord! Derrick, it's my friend, Ives." She pulled me inside and smothered me in a hug. Her white silk pajamas and matching duster dried and soothed my face.

I wanted to invite Janene in out of the drenching rain, but Rosa Leigh was taking her time embracing me. When she got around to releasing me from her bear hug, she motioned Janene inside and eased the door shut. "This must be your boss."

I cringed. "This is my partner. And who is the dark, handsome young man holding the baseball bat?"

"Derrick Little," he said, lowering his weapon. "Gram's grandson."

Janene interrupted my get-acquainted-moment. "Ms. Adams, please accept my apologies for arriving early." Her cold eyes glowered at me. "Ives assured me that coming a day before you'd planned would please you."

"Oh my, it does! We," she said, swirling her hand to include herself and her grandson, "are a bit skittish here since Derrick found the cave, and we discovered the skull. Lots of strange things have been happening. The road is hot with cars, and I hear noises at night. The Sheriff says the traffic is due to an increase in drugs around here. But, I think someone wants to scare us so we won't look for the skull."

Rosa Leigh stopped twittering on about her theories and then stooped to pick up Janene's suitcase. "Come with me. You must be tired and hungry. I'll show you where you'll be staying. I think you'll find the mother-in-law quarters quiet, and the scenery of the lake and the mountain will be inspiring for novel writing."

I'm left standing with my suitcase in hand, and I'm miffed.

Derrick smiled and swept his hand toward the great room with its cathedral ceiling. "Make yourself comfortable, Ms. Schnepe. My Gram will probably talk your friend to sleep before she returns."

A giant Golden Retriever appeared from around the corner and rubbed against my leg. He sniffed my shoes and peered up at me, almost grinning.

"Please sit," Derrick said, motioning to a white sofa.

I set my suitcase down and did as he wished.

Half a lifetime later, Rosa Leigh reappeared, flushed and smelling of expensive perfume. She rushed towards me, arms open. "Ives, I can't believe you're here." She smothered me in another tight hug and rocked us side-to-side.

I wanted to catch up with her and all that was going on, but I was famished. "Where's your kitchen, Rosa Leigh?"

She walked me arm-in-arm down a short hall into a dining area. I scanned the walls, lined with family photos, all beautiful and handsome faces, with one exception…Rosa Leigh's father. He had always given the impression that he was suffering from serious hemorrhoids.

As I finished perusing the photos, I thought about Rosa Leigh's history. She was raised in poverty but somehow rose out of the swamp. At one time, she was all about power, and she didn't care how she gained it.

I smoothed my wrinkled, floral blouse, rolled my tired shoulders and entered her kitchen. The yellow walls were bright and reflected my friend's sunny personality.

"What's to eat?" I asked.

Rosa Leigh scratched her head. "Let's look. Derrick and I ate at Nettie's Café, and we didn't bring any leftovers home."

He opened the refrigerator door and gazed inside.

My stomach grumbled. I nudged him aside, rummaged through a drawer and pulled out a roll of Kentucky Border bologna. Placing the meat on the counter, I found a loaf of French bread.

I glanced at Derrick, who was watching me with a mix of awe and disbelief.

"Your grandmother and I have always had a taste for fried baloney," I said. "We like it almost burned with the edges crispy. Want some?"

He shook his head.

"Young man, you don't know what you're missing. I'll fix Janene one. When she smells it, she'll be here," I said, opening doors and drawers until I found a skillet.

I placed the cast iron on the burner, sliced a hunk of meat, slapped it in the pan and peeled an onion while the meat sizzled. The wonderful aroma floated through the air, and my mouth watered. When the edges were brown and curled, I forked it onto a slice of bread, covered it with ringlets of a sweet onion, popped the top on and crunched into the scrumptious delicacy.

"Nowhere else can you find a great sandwich like this," I said, my words garbled as I kept eating while I was talking. "Tell me, Derrick, about this skull you found. Is it an adult? Oh geez, tell me it's not a child. And tell me why the local police haven't jumped on this with both feet."

"The Sheriff wants me to lead him to the spot," Derrick said and rubbed his nose. "But I haven't been able to find it again. The area is on a mountainside with heavy shrubs and trees."

"I've lived here twenty years, Ives, and didn't know the cave was there. We've never done a controlled burn like our neighbors," Rosa Leigh said and shrugged. "Derrick can't find it because it's like hiking through a wilderness up there."

"I wouldn't have found it if I hadn't been bored last Sunday and went for a hike. I've tried to retrace my steps twice. Once by myself mid-week and another time with my dad and mom last weekend. We couldn't find the cave."

I wiped my mouth with a napkin. "As soon as the sun dries the dew in the morning, you and I will explore again." I patted Derrick's knee and turned to Rosa Leigh. "Do you want to go?"

Her hand flew to her chest. "Absolutely not! You know I'm terrified of snakes, and they didn't pull the name Copperhead Ridge out of the air. This hollow is crawling with those devils, so you two be careful."

"We will. I brought some jeans and long sleeve shirts, but I'll need to borrow a pair of boots or good hiking shoes."

"You know you can wear mine," Rosa Leigh said and smiled. "We've always traded shoes. I'll find some for you. You'll need my walking stick, too. In these snake-infested parts, you want to beat the bushes and shrubs ahead of you—before you walk. You've been gone so long, I'm sure you don't remember all these techniques." She motioned for me to follow her down the hall to a closet in the foyer.

I carried my half-eaten sandwich with me.

She handed me a pair of hiking boots. "I remember how impatient you are, old friend, but you've got to be aware of your surroundings. Listen for rustling leaves and grass and check the air for smells of cucumbers. Copperheads smell like the vegetable."

I nodded. "Thanks for the reminder. I forgot about their odor."

"There's lots you don't remember about this area, I would imagine," Rosa Leigh said, putting her arm around my shoulder and leading me towards the bedroom I'd be sleeping in.

I carried a pair of boots in one hand and my food in the other. I glanced over my shoulder and called out, "Good night, Derrick."

He waved and walked into the family room.

Following my friend, I asked, "Who do you think the skull belongs to?"

Rosa Leigh shrugged. "Two years ago, one of the local high school boys didn't make it home one night. The next day, the police found his car. The front doors were open, and blood was on the passenger seat. The lakes and ponds were dragged, hollows and ravines searched, but he was never found. His disappearance is still an open case."

I plopped my suitcase on the bed. As I unpacked, Rosa Leigh reminisced, but I was too tired and preoccupied with the skull to pay any attention to what she was saying. I set the empty luggage in the closet and lay on the bed. Rosa Leigh was still talking.

In the wee hours, I awoke to find her curled on the other side of my bed.

I could hardly wait until daylight. Convinced Derrick and I would find the mysterious cave and the skull, I turned over, thinking about what it all might mean. Butterflies fluttered in my stomach.

Janene is afraid I'll get into trouble, but everyone wants this mystery solved. And that's what we're here to do. What could happen just going on a hike?

Chapter 3

Rosa Leigh and I woke up at 6:00 A.M, stumbled into the kitchen and brewed coffee. Neither one of us talked much until the caffeine fired our brain cells. I continued the trip back in time we had begun last night. Chatting about the past made it all seem like yesterday. When Janene interrupted an hour later, I bristled.

"Cereal's in the top right cupboard," Rosa Leigh said and pointed to it.

Janene wrinkled her nose.

"English Muffins, bagels and cream cheese or cut up fresh fruit are in the refrigerator. The only time we have hot breakfasts is when we go to the restaurant."

Janene decided on a bagel with a thin layer of blackberry jam.

"Nettie Stamper picked the berries, made the jam and gave a jar to me for Christmas," Rosa Leigh said, "I have a pint of raspberry jelly in the pantry, too, if you want it."

Janene took a bite, closed her eyes and moaned. She slid onto the bar stool next to me, and the aroma of the delicious fruit and bagel reached my nose.

I studied Rosa Leigh. "As much canning and jelly making you did as a girl, I'm surprised you don't preserve your own."

"Number one, too much work," she said, ticking off that reason on her finger before moving onto another one and another finger. "Two, I can afford to buy it. But the main reason is, I wouldn't go into the snake-infested fields and woods to pick berries unless I was starving."

I nudged Janene and winked. "She's grown soft."

"Don't let Ives taunt you," Janene said. "She probably hasn't hiked here since she was young." She turned towards a sound coming from a room off the hall. "Your grandson's snoring?"

Rosa Leigh nodded. "Sounds like a freight train sometimes."

We laughed.

Simon, Rosa Leigh's Golden Retriever, rose from his corner, walked to Rosa Leigh and placed his snout on her leg.

"Are you feeling left out?" She stroked his neck. "Come on."

As dog food clinked into his bowl, Rosa Leigh drifted into the past again.

Janene listened until the last sip of coffee. After she put her plate and cup in the dishwasher, she said, "The desk in front of the giant window is calling. I plan to be dressed and working by 8:00 until my manuscript is done." She walked across the kitchen. "What are the dinner plans?"

"I thought Ives would enjoy the experience at the local restaurant. She probably will run into a few old friends."

I nodded, thrilled with the idea. "How's 6:00 sound? Will you have enough writing time?"

"I'm quitting at 5:00 every day. The inviting pool and the paddle boat on the big lake look like fun."

"There are two jet skis in the shed, too. I look forward to racing you," Rosa Leigh said.

"You're on," Janene said and waved over her shoulder. "See you at dinner."

I showered, dressed and took a seat on a bar stool at the kitchen island waiting for Derrick to wake up. At 9:00, he staggered into the room yawning.

"About time you're up," I teased. "I thought about going without you."

A sheepish grin spread across his face. "This is my last day to sleep late, Ms. Schnepe. I start two-a-days in football camp tomorrow." He pulled down a box of cereal, and after filling a bowl, sat at the table, bowed his head and said a silent grace.

"Haven't seen anyone bless their food in a long time," I said, glancing at Rosa Leigh. "Your grandmother and I once did. It's been so long ago it never enters my mind these days."

"Do you go to church?" Derrick asked.

"Every Sunday."

He glanced at his grandmother. "Gram likes to sleep in, except when I'm here."

She scrunched her lips.

I let it go and nodded toward the dog. "Is he going hiking with us?"

Derrick chuckled. "Try going outside without him. Besides, he's a good snake detector. His keen sense of smell and hearing is light years ahead of us." Derrick placed his empty bowl in the dishwasher. "I won't take long." His voice trailed off as he disappeared down the hallway.

I slipped into the borrowed hiking boots and filled my backpack with food and water for three. I lifted the bag. "Too heavy," I said to Rosa Leigh. "Derrick will carry his own supplies. I haven't hiked a mountainside since I was a kid, and even then, it was grueling."

"Keep an eye out for intruders. Copperheads aren't the only snakes in this hollow. There are a few two-legged ones deadlier than those slithering on their bellies," Rosa Leigh warned.

I thought about the reception we'd received the night before. "You once were afraid of guns and now you own one. Do you know how to use it?"

Rosa Leigh sank into a chair. "Yes, I took gun safety lessons, thank you very much, and I have a license to carry. But, I don't. During the day, I lock it in a safe. I take it out at bedtime, or when someone scares me. Like I said before, too many people skulking around outside looking for a way to break in. One of these times, one will manage the task, and I intend to defend myself. Amendment 2 says I have the right to own a gun, and a right to protect myself against those who carry bigger ones. If it weren't for Simon, I'd be terrified. If there are sounds, he wakes me. There's a security system, but everyone knows the police need a good twenty to twenty-five minutes to drive here."

"Why don't you ask for the police to patrol the road?"

"Because they don't have enough manpower to cover all the break-ins. They're occurring all around here."

"It's certainly not the old neighborhood I remember. No one locked their door back then."

"They do now," Rosa Leigh said and harrumphed.

Derrick entered the room dressed in jeans, a long sleeve denim shirt and a red cap with the Kentucky Wildcat logo on it. "Are you ready, Ms. Schnepe?"

"My friends call me Ives, and I include you on that list."

Derrick grinned and opened the back door. Simon scurried out, and I followed. Derrick brought up the rear.

I didn't need a thermometer to tell me it was stifling hot. Not a leaf or a blade of grass stirred as we walked past the lake towards the foothill. The smell of dry grass hung in the air. A green dragonfly swooped down, circled the water and flew away. Black mud daubers worked the slippery bank. Simon chased a red-breasted robin to a low hanging branch, took a peek back at us and started into the water.

"No, Boy!" Derrick yelled.

Simon waded into the water up to his underside and grinned. As we walked by him, he bounded out and trotted next to Derrick. He shook, the fishy smelling lake water showering us.

Within five minutes, we were at the bottom of the tall mountain. Shrubs, bushes, thorns and vines grew thick at the edge.

I whacked the thicket in front of me and said, "Rosa Leigh should have these trees thinned so new ones can grow."

"She let a guy log one year. He cut all white oak. Gram knows her trees, and when he came off the mountain, she checked his load, and told him he was finished cutting on her property."

"So, how high up the mountain were you the day you found the cave?" I asked, letting the tree-thinning conversation go.

"Not too high," Derrick said, parting a tall clump of grass. "Once we are farther up where the leaves are thick, there'll be less brush and undergrowth." His words trailed over his shoulder. "Use your walking stick to test the ground in front of you before you step, Ms. Ives. I nearly fell into a ravine the other day. It was hidden beneath a patch of growth. Be careful of big rocks, too. It hurts if you trip."

He stopped and wiped his forehead. "I'm starting football practice with a scabbed knee, and it'll be knocked off first drill," he said and laughed.

Simon weaved around shrubs and high-stepped to loosen a vine tugging his back leg. It broke off, and he was then able to jump over a dead tree lying in his path.

"Onward and upward, if we want to keep up with the snake detector," I said and shivered, remembering the warnings I'd received as a toddler about the danger. "Snakes like to sun themselves on logs and rocks because they are cold-blooded. We stand a big chance of seeing one on this hot day."

Derrick poked the ground in front of him with his stick and shrugged.

Goosebumps prickled on my neck.

Tangles of briars and bushes snagged our skin. Squirrels chattered, birds chirped, and dry leaves rustled beneath our shoes.

After what seemed like many hours, but was probably just a couple, we grew tired and hungry. I tossed Derrick a bologna sandwich and Simon a strip of beef jerky. Both devoured them within seconds, and I let them drink water while I enjoyed mine. When I finished, I collected the trash, and we set off again.

We trekked up and wound around the mountain until my calf muscles began to cramp. There wasn't one sign of a cave. Finally, Derrick looked at his watch and said, "My dad is picking me up after work today. He may be waiting."

I sighed a long breath. "I thought you were never going to stop."

He laughed. "Unlike my first hike, in which I broke limbs or bent saplings every few feet to be able to retrace our steps, I didn't plan to return before, so it didn't occur to me to mark a trail."

I nudged his shoulder. "Who's going to guide me up and down this mountainside when you're not available?"

He nodded to Simon. "He will. He hunts these woods every time Gram lets him out, and he drops his catch on the patio in front of her French door," Derrick said and chuckled.

"You're the one who found the cave, not Simon," I said, not sure I was comfortable with it just being me and Simon.

"He was hiking with me. He'll be good company, and if he disappears, it won't be for long."

We started down the mountain, Simon leading, followed by Derrick and then me.

An afternoon of sweat, scratches and sore muscles, and nothing to show for it. It's like a jungle up here.

Chapter 4

Rosa Leigh, Janene and I arrived at Nettie's at 6:30 P.M.

The restaurant is a large, cozy cottage, Norman Rockwell style, with a tall Kentucky mountain in the background. At the entrance, people rocked in rustic twig rockers on a wrap-around porch. Rosa Leigh walked through the door first and was escorted to a table at the back.

As we followed, the aromas of grilled steak and coffee made my mouth water. Sounds of silverware scraping plates, laughter and pieces of conversations filled the room. Electric candles flickered on the cloth-covered tables.

As soon as we were seated, a bouncy waitress with red hair placed menus on the table and asked for our drink orders. When she left, Rosa Leigh nudged my arm and hitched her head. "Do you recognize the person strolling to the table by the window?"

A man whose black hair was streaked with silver caught my eye. My heart skipped a beat. The years had wrinkled the corner of his eyes, and his jowls sagged a bit. Though his brow had a permanent furrow, his eyes were still the brilliant blue I remembered from high school.

A police uniform replaced the jeans and t-shirt of his former days. As he pulled out the chair for his lady friend, my words come out in a whisper, "Blake Sheets."

Rosa Leigh stared longingly at him. "Still a handsome hunk for his age."

"Who did he marry?"

"Hilda Sparks. She passed away five years ago, and yes, he's available."

I swat at the air. "Like I'm interested after all these years."

"This isn't just any man," Rosa Leigh said and poked my arm with her index finger. "He's the one you dated for three years during high school, and he asked you to marry him."

Janene leaned in close. "Juicy facts. Rosa Leigh, fill in the gaps." She straightened in her seat to get a better view and nodded approvingly. "I never met your late husband, Ives, but he must have been extra special to take this man's place."

"Blake and Ives won king and queen of the junior and senior proms. Everyone thought they would be married after graduation, but Ives knew what she wanted. She couldn't talk him into going to college with her, and she knew education was her ticket out of here," Rosa Leigh said, sipping her iced lemon water and dabbing her lips before continuing. "We both knew college was our ticket. We were inseparable during high school and college, until she met her engineer. He swept her off her feet." She chuckled. "And I'd say seven children and married to the same man until death turned out to be a great match."

I sighed, knowing how right Rosa Leigh was. "I loved Blake, but he and I were always on different wavelengths. He couldn't imagine living anywhere else." I leaned back in my chair. "His family was more prosperous than mine. Dad was a coal miner for years, and when the mines closed, he logged. He barely managed to feed and clothe us."

I glimpsed movement out of the corner of my eye and turned. Our waitress had returned with our orders, accompanied by an older lady with short, curly gray hair. A plate of steaming food was placed in front of me. I leaned over it and let the aroma of beef and gravy whet my appetite.

"Hello, my old friend."

I pulled my head up from the delectable food, and my mouth gaped. "Oh, my goodness! Nettie Stamper is it really you?" I jumped up, and we clung to each other. I tried to pull away, but Nettie held me tight.

"You were in my dreams last night," she whispered into my ear. "You be careful. Evil angels are lurking in these parts, and they're watching you."

As I stepped back to introduce Nettie to Janene, my skin tingled. The two traded formal greetings, and then Nettie glared at Rosa Leigh. "What you're asking her to do is dangerous."

Rosa Leigh rubbed her palms across her capris. "Oh, Nettie. Ives is visiting after forty years away. Now you stop talking nonsense."

Nettie pointed her finger at Rosa Leigh. "You know I've only been wrong once."

A cold streak slithered up my spine. I shivered.

Nettie's eyes darted from me to Janene. "You ladies will be at Rosa Leigh's card game tomorrow night, I assume?"

"Of course, they will," Rosa Leigh said. "They're my house guests. And if they want to come Wednesday to help with Art on Wheels at The Country Club Retirement Home, they can do that, too."

Nettie folded her arms across her chest. "Miss Ramsey, I can't wait to buy your book. Rosa Leigh tells me it's called, *Abandoned in the Everglades*. I love cozy mysteries. Will you sign it for me?"

Janene's eyes opened wide. She gulped her bite of food and said, "It will be my pleasure."

"Enjoy your dinners," Nettie said and left our table.

I forked a bite of beef tips over egg noodles into my watering mouth and moaned. "I haven't tasted anything this delicious since my momma died."

"Nettie serves some of the dishes our mothers once prepared," Rosa Leigh said, and turned her head to read from a dry erase board. "Monday's menu includes pinto beans with smoked ham." She turned back to us. "I love pinto beans with smoked ham, fried potatoes and corn bread. Fried pork chops, potatoes and red eye gravy like your mother used to fix, are on for Tuesday." Rosa Leigh curled her fingers to touch her thumb on one hand, placed them to her lips and made a smacking sound.

"Heart attack food," Janene said.

I laughed. "We Kentuckians invented roux and bread dipping. Nothing better if you have a buttermilk biscuit, too. It's a good thing those beans were good for us. My family certainly ate enough of them. Dad wanted pinto beans, fried potatoes and biscuits every day."

Rosa Leigh placed her fork on her plate. "Remember the apple butter stack cake my momma made?"

I nodded.

She clapped her hands with glee. "It's on the Monday menu, too!"

"Does Nettie make her mother's famous coconut cake?" I asked, so hoping she did.

"It's on today's menu, girlfriend, and she bakes her mother's apple and blackberry pie recipe. Nettie has someone else bake some of the desserts, but she cooks all the meats and side dishes."

I smiled. "She always said one day she would own a restaurant. She's one of the few classmates who knew what they wanted to do when we graduated. I'm happy for her. Did she marry?"

Rosa Leigh clucked her tongue. "With her unusual gift, the boys were afraid of her after our junior year when she blabbed about seeing Rick Bolton at the bottom of the lake, and three weeks later, the police found him there."

Janene pushed her plate away. "Your friend will make a great book character for paranormal readers. Are dreams the only way she sees the future?" She asked, winking at me. "I heard what she whispered into your ear."

"In this area, her gift . . .," I said, cocking my eyebrow, "or curse, is called having second sight. I don't know how she knows. She's normal and fun to be around most of the time." I sipped my lemon water then continued, "Nettie's folks were extremely superstitious. Mine, too. Mom used to toss salt over her shoulder if she spilled it, and she would almost panic if she saw a black cat." I closed my eyes as I thought about her more curious ideas. "And…she believed bad things happened in three's."

"Most were superstitious back then," Rosa Leigh added. "And had crazy ideas. If my grandmother was canning peaches, she wouldn't let us touch them if either of us were on our monthlies. She said it caused them to rot."

I laughed. "We'd lie to her, telling her we were and go swimming."

Rosa Leigh's comment about peaches rotting reminded me of pickled foods. "Does Nettie serve pickled corn and beans and those mixed vegetables her mother called *piccalilli*?"

Rosa Leigh nodded. "It's a delicacy to some of the old timers. We don't have many who order that dish now."

Rosa Leigh scooted her chair from the table. "I have to catch Blake before he's out the door."

A few minutes later, Blake swaggered across the room, his arm around my friend's shoulder. I smoothed my wiry gray hair and extended my hand as he walked near.

He pulled me to my feet and wrapped me in his muscular arms.

Oh, this feels like home. He smells spicy and clean, like the woods, and oh so good. After all these years, he still wears Avon's Wild Country cologne. I gave him his first bottle our first Christmas.

Blake released me and stepped back. Smiling, his warm eyes scanned from my head to my toes. "You're still a beautiful woman. Time's been good to you."

My cheeks burned. "And you still know what a woman wants to hear." I stared deep into his gorgeous eyes. "Time's been better to you."

And then we stared at each other, silent, like two tongue-tied teenagers.

"She'll be here a while, Blake, if you want to catch up, call my house," Rosa Leigh said, spoiling the moment.

I smacked her forearm.

He chuckled. "I want to know all about your life. May I call you?"

I nodded.

He glanced toward the window. "I have to go. I don't want to leave my friend sitting alone while I talk to three gorgeous women." His eyes darted from me to Rosa Leigh and Janene. "Is this your daughter, Ives?"

Janene offered her hand. "Janene Ramsey. We're here to investigate the skull in the cave photo. Ives told me she knew the Chief of Police. I wasn't expecting the connection to be this close."

He twirled his hat on his finger. "You have to find the cave first, and then I'll be glad to assist."

He bumped my shoulder. "It'll be fun traipsing around the mountainside with you again." He winked and walked away.

Rosa Leigh sat back down in her chair. "Whether you find the cave or not, Ives, you might light the simmering coals."

"I was thinking the same thing," Janene said, curling a strand of brown hair around her finger.

My heart thumped against my chest.

Chapter 5

The next morning, as daylight crept over the mountain, I awoke. I drank my usual two cups of coffee, ate a bowl of oatmeal and fed Simon. While he ate, I packed a lunch, including his dog treats, for the laborious trek up the mountain. I wrote a brief note telling the ladies the general direction I was heading and left before they could slow me down with morning chit chat.

As I passed the lake, a breeze wafted by, filling my nose with the fishy smell of the water. Dew drops, like clear gems, glistened off the grass blades and soaked my borrowed hiking boots. Chirps, peeps and caws echoing back and forth filled the warm air. I recognized a few of the singers perching in the branches: a blue jay, a red bird and a crow—who sounded a warning as I approached.

Simon chased all flying things, and I almost tumbled over him when a jar fly buzzed my face. I missed Derrick and his occasional conversation.

With only the soothing sounds of nature mingled with the hush of my footsteps, I stopped to enjoy the moment. *No sirens trilling, no humming engines and no honking horns. I can become accustomed to this way of life again.*

When we approach the tree line, Simon barked, and darted toward a clump of tall grass. He backed away, circled it and charged. I ran towards him. *Don't let it be a copperhead or a rattlesnake this early in the day.*

I stopped three or four feet from the dog, took a deep breath and inched closer. A chipmunk scurried out of his hiding place. I jumped and blew out the breath I'd been holding. "Leave it! Save your energy for a catch worthy of your size," I said, nudging him with my leg, so we could trudge on.

The smell of pine and moldy vegetation filled the air beneath the trees. An occasional drop of water splattered the top of my head from the overhead branches. Glancing often to the saplings on my right, I made certain the broken and bent twigs from the last trip were visible, listened for a rattling from a rattlesnake and sniffed often for the cucumber smell of a copperhead. Simon ran up the mountain ahead of me with an energy I envied. An ache sizzled up my thighs and doubt pounded my brain.

I stopped and scanned the area. *What made me think I could find a cave on this mountain?* My calves throbbed, and I was out of breath. I kneaded the back of my legs. *I'm in no shape for this trek.* I pivoted and scanned the area, again. *At least there are no large predators like bears or bobcats in these parts—no recent sightings anyway.*

A sudden gust of wind whistled through the tree nearest me and startled me. I shuddered and whacked at a clump of green briars blocking the way. The vines began to vibrate, and the dried leaves beneath them rustled. Two brown blurs scuttled near my feet, and my blood-curdling scream echoed through the air. I eased left and stepped across a bunch of ferns, wishing the mountain had hiking trails.

Gram and I once traipsed these hills hunting ginseng, "seng" as she called it, and yellow root. She cleaned and hung the plants to dry until she'd had enough to take to market. Remembering our good times, I smiled.

I wonder if the old white oak is standing in the back yard of the home place? Oh my, the stories we children heard as we strung and broke beans beneath the shade of the tree. Memories continued to flow from the crevices of my mind.

I parted a bunch of tall weeds, waited, and when nothing ventured out, I ambled on. The further I climbed, the hotter the air, and the more work hiking became. I pushed upward until my legs turned into one constant ache. Finally, I stopped to massage the small of my back.

A rabbit jumped out from beneath shrubs, Simon barked, and the bunny bounced away with Simon chasing it.

"Come here," I yelled, waving beef jerky through the air. While I waited for him, I found a spot without shrubs and briars to sit for lunch. When he returned, I tossed him his treat. He caught it mid-air. I laughed and glanced at my watch. It was 12:15. "Buddy, we're almost to the top and not a sign of a cave. We're quitting."

He chewed his treat and stared at me as if he understood.

"It's going to be eighty-four degrees by afternoon, if it isn't all ready, and there's no breeze." I swiped beads of sweat from my forehead, using the back of my hand, and took another bite of my bologna sandwich. "You and I are going to visit the old cemetery Rosa Leigh told me about last night. Some of my relatives may be buried there."

Simon gulped the last of his food and grinned.

"Sorry. You ate all I brought." I wadded up the sandwich bag, put it inside my backpack and took out a plastic whipped cream container. He lapped at the stream of water as I poured it into the container. I stroked his reddish-orange head.

On the way down the mountain, I traveled within sight of my trail markings, and made new ones, so I could search again tomorrow without retracing my steps. We made better time going down-hill. Still, the afternoon shadows stretched from the trees almost to the lake.

I followed the foothills to the highway and walked east. When I crossed the ditch-line to the road, the shade disappeared. After a few yards, Simon stopped in the middle of the pavement and stared behind me. A red, four-wheel-drive truck sped our way.

"Come here, boy," I yelled.

As the tires hummed closer, and the engine roared louder, he continued staring at the vehicle.

I clapped my hands. He glanced my way then looked back at the truck and grinned.

"Out of the way, stupid!" I screamed, running to him and yanking him to the gravel at the side of the highway.

Stones crunched beneath the wide tires. The driver honked. SWISH! He passed and left us in a trail of dust.

Simon jerked lose and chased the vehicle, nipping at the wheels as the man sped away. The dog pranced back to me, panting. I cupped his face in my hands and said, "Bad dog!"

He pulled his snout lose and trotted away, head held high as if he'd defeated the canine monster every dog searched for.

We arrived minutes later at the cemetery located on the west side of the highway. The weathered wooden gate was unlocked, and we walked in. Like sentinels guarding the dead, several tall birch trees stood in a row in the middle. Three paw-paw fruit trees edged part of the east side. I strolled the rows, fingered the rough stones and read the names. Some markers were tall and ornate, others short and plain, and a few were marked with metal crosses.

I recognized Rosa Leigh's parents' headstone markers and a few of her uncles and aunts. Several of the tall tombstones dated back to the 1800's, but most were placed there during World War I and II. The short, squat ones were more recent, however. I didn't see any of my relations, and after checking each monument, I led Simon to a pond across the road.

A bench sat on the east side of the water and faced the cemetery. I strolled through the tall grass and had a seat. Simon waded into water up to his belly and stood there with an "aww-that-feels-good" look on his face.

"Good afternoon."

I jumped and whirled around.

A frail, thin woman hobbled towards me, placing most of her weight on a four-pronged cane. Her wrinkly skin hung loosely on her bones. "You found my favorite place." She smiled, dropped onto the seat, and nodded towards the cemetery.

"My husband's over there. Sometimes, I walk across the road and talk to him." She took a laced-trimmed handkerchief out of her pocket, blew her nose and dabbed at her eyes brimming with tears. "Copperhead Ridge has so much traffic these days I'm afraid to walk across the pavement by myself." She stuck out her bony hand. "Mertle Overstreet." Jerking her thumb over her shoulder, she said, "I live through those trees."

I shook her sweaty palm, told her my name and the names of my parents, Ned and Ivannele Lambert.

The woman nodded. "I remember them. They're buried over on Red Brush, aren't they?"

"They are."

She smiled and asked, "Where did you wander off to when you graduated high school?"

"Palmetto, Florida, on the Gulf Coast. I married my college sweetheart, and his engineer job took us there. I'm here to visit my childhood friend, Rosa Leigh Adams."

"Fine woman," Mertle said and pointed to the cemetery. "A lot of her folks are buried over there. See the rows of gorgeous birch? Her dad planted those and the three paw-paws." She gazed at me. "Did you ever eat a ripe paw-paw?"

"A long time ago."

"No finer fruit, sweet and juicy, but hard to pick. They ripen after the first frost, and within two or three days, they turn black. We always tried to beat the groundhogs and raccoons to them." Mertle looked towards the cemetery, once more.

"Have you lived here long?" I asked.

She swatted at a wasp. "Born here, and oh the tales I can tell about this ridge." She chuckled and pointed to the mountain behind us. "My father taught my husband how to make white lightning. The still is somewhere up there. My dad bootlegged for years, until the revenue men became thicker than flies in these hills. He hid out in the woods for three weeks once. Them G-men hunted the whole time but never found him." She paused, appearing to be lost in her memories.

I cleared my throat.

"My husband found a job on the railroad and made a good living. When he died, we bought this house and raised three fine boys and a girl. Danita joined me few years back when her husband was killed in Iraq."

Simon barked, startling Mertle. "Guess he wants us to pay attention to him. Did Rosa Leigh tell you the legend about what might've been hidden in the pond?"

"No," I said, my mind thinking about the still she mentioned.

"As the story goes, someone's relative robbed a jewelry store in Columbus, Ohio, and hid out in these mountains for months. Supposedly, they stashed a bag in the pond for safe keeping." Mertle giggled. "Every boy 'round here's searched the murky green water for those jewels. Either the robbers escaped with them," she turned to face me, "or someone else found them. No one found the jewelry, and the thieves were never caught." She leaned forward and scratched her leg.

"Have you ever been to the cave on the mountain behind us?" I asked.

"Nope, but I know there's one up there. At one time, it linked with the Carter Cave system, but with all the cave-ins, I doubt it does now." She fanned her face. "Whew, lands its hot. Someone needs to plant one shade tree near this bench. There's a legend about the cave, too, you know."

I opened a bottle of water, and as I handed it to her, I said, "Tell me, please."

After she swallowed a long drink, she thanked me and said, "Should carry my own in this heat. My daughter will be furious if she discovers I've walked here while she was grocery shopping." She handed the water back. "Give the rest to the pretty dog. He's panting like he needs a drink."

Though he probably drank from the pond, I took the whipped cream container out of the backpack and poured the remainder of the water into it as she began to share the legend…

"One of the Indian men who once roamed these hills fell in love with a local girl, and they planned to meet and disappear into the mountains with his people. He knew the cave had silver in it, because his tribe made trinkets from it. The two love birds set a time to meet, and he went to the cave with his tools. He made a beautiful necklace." Mertle leaned her head to the side and closed her eyes. "Or was it a bracelet?"

Her eyes opened. "I can't remember. Anyway, while he was there working on the piece, there was a cave-in, and he was trapped inside and never seen again. The girl went to the meeting site, but he didn't show. Local lore says she never married. When she was an old woman, a prospector decided to check out the silver theory, and dug through the collapsed rock in the cave. When he returned, he had a piece of beautiful jewelry, and he told the town folk he'd found it in the hand of a skeleton. The bride-to-be's heart leapt with joy. All those years she thought her Indian warrior jilted her."

Mertle slapped at a gnat on her leg. "Near here, there's reportedly a cave full of silver. People from all over the country have searched, but never found the cave. Guess no one will find it until the mountain topples." She scooted forward on the bench, rocked back and forth several times and stood. "I better be going." She waved. "Maybe we'll see each other again."

She disappeared into the trees, and I left for home.

When I opened the back door, Janene rushed towards me. "Where have you been?"

Rosa Leigh massaged her temples. "We were going to call a search party if you weren't here by five. You haven't changed a bit. You still don't pay attention to time."

Janene folded her arms beneath her breast. "Rosa Leigh's friends will be here at six to play cards, and you promised to join them."

I looked at the clock on the microwave. It was 4:55, so I scurried down the hall.

Chapter 6

By the time Simon and I reached the three tall ferns at the bottom of the mountain the next morning, the autumn air was stifling hot. The wind fluttered the leaves at the top of the trees, but not a blade of grass stirred at ground level. I pounded the vegetation to scare the snakes out, and the smell of fresh grass filled the air. When nothing rushed out at me, I ventured on.

Inside the woods, Simon took the lead, and before long, we walked upon a swatch of the hillside recently logged. The vegetation hadn't grown back. Judging by the tree stumps jutting up, the person doing the logging lacked knowledge about forestry. He'd cut all the trees, including the pine. I was certain Rosa Leigh wouldn't let him strip the land.

As I trudged on, a high cloud scuttled in front of the sun and blocked the hot rays, giving a welcoming shadow. The continued absence of sirens, train whistles and honking horns reminded me how much I loved the area before high school and my longing for new adventures. I don't know how long we climbed, but when my tongue stuck to the roof of my mouth, I stopped for lunch.

I called Simon, waved his beef jerky, and he sauntered back. I tossed the treat, and it disappeared in the tall grass near him. He gazed at me, his tongue lolling, but made no effort to hunt the food. I set a plastic container on the ground and poured his water. He lapped up all the water before he sniffed the grass for his lunch, and I gulped half a bottle before I bit into a peanut butter and jelly sandwich.

Even the forest creatures were quiet in the sweltering August heat. I leaned my head against a hickory tree and dozed, but when Simon whined, I was jarred awake. He licked the back of my hand and glanced up the mountain.

My stomach quivered. "Did you hear something?"

He squinted at me but didn't budge. Looking all around, I pushed my sandwich back into the baggie, jammed it back in my pack and stood. Simon's ears were perked, but he wasn't in any hurry to investigate. For a second, or two, I considered going to the house, but curiosity won. I crept upward.

With Simon staying only a few feet in front of me, every nerve in my body was on high alert. When two male voices boomed through the air, and a loud sound like metal against rock echoed through the leaves, he stopped. Despite the mugginess, I shivered and grabbed Simon's collar to keep him from darting ahead. He growled.

When I stepped forward, a thorny vine snagged my leg. Plummeting forward, I grabbed the rough bark of an oak. Pain shot through my palm, and I blew on my hand until the burn eased and I could walk higher.

The pounding stopped, and the voices grew louder.

A guttural growl escaped from Simon.

Still holding his collar, I tiptoed several steps, hid behind a white oak and peered around its trunk.

When I saw two men carrying sacks into a cave, the nape of my neck tingled.

I waited for their voices to fade. When the roar in my ears subsided, I inched my head around the trunk again.

Large pieces of shale laid sporadically along the small, dried-up creek bed leading to the opening. Two large trees and several small saplings grew on one side of the entrance.

On top, a mason jar lay on its side, half full of leaves and dirt. A long walking stick was next to it. To the left, a tall pole was stuck in the ground, and a tattered remnant of a colored rag or bandana drooped from the top.

I looked further left, and the air gushed from my lungs.

The skull, partially blocked by dead leaves and twigs, was there, propped against a tree.

Until Simon nudged my thigh and knocked me out of my frozen state, I was rooted to the ground. I stroked his neck, snatched my phone from my back pocket and snapped photos of the site.

Simon growled again.

"Okay, boy. I agree. It's time to leave."

Voices echoed off the walls inside the cave. I bolted back out of sight and leaned against the tree until my ragged breaths slowed. When I peered back around, Simon was standing in view of the cave, watching. I raced to him, grabbed his collar and yanked him to safety.

"Now is not the time to act brave," I whispered.

I took another quick peek around the tree and saw a burly man with black hair and a bushy mustache standing in the entrance. A short, wiry man trailed him. As the first one studied the area, his cold brown eyes darted from side-to-side.

I placed my phone against the tree bark, snapped a photo and yanked the phone back, hoping I got a good shot.

The man's head jerked our way. "Did you hear something?"

The other man cupped his hand around his ear. "Rustling leaves . . .maybe. The wind's picked up a little."

"Probably," the first man said. He observed the sky. "Storm clouds rollin' in." He pointed to the path where Simon and I were just a few minutes earlier. "Let's go. I want off this mountainside before the rain comes."

As they tramped down the slope, dry leaves crunched, and twigs snapped within two feet of the copse of trees and shrubbery in which we are hiding.

"It's a long way down, and other than the trees, there's no hiding place. We have to descend without making a sound," I whispered to Simon, so glad he was there with me.

He snuggled closer.

When I no longer heard the men's voices, I stepped out from our hiding place, holding Simon's collar to keep him from charging after them. Noticing his desire to stay near me and his lack of a whimper, I decided I had nothing to worry about. He must have been wishing to stay out of their way, too.

I took several more photos of the area and then tucked my phone into my hip pocket. To make room for the treasures we'd discovered, I took the whipped cream container, water bottle, and half-eaten sandwich out of my backpack and stashed it beneath a clump of grass where no one could see it. Weighing it down with a rock, I knew it would be there the next trip.

I ran to the skull, bent to pick it up, but then yanked my hands away. At the thought of handling someone's bones with my bare hands, an icy-chill shot through my veins.

Before I could formulate a plan, however, I heard feet stomping through the nearby bushes.

My churning stomach flip flopped.

Simon's eyes were locked in the direction of the rustling, and his hackles were raised. I whispered in his ear, "Don't bark. Don't make a sound."

We raced back to the same copse of white oak and hunkered down.

A clean-shaven man, with hair so dark it reflected navy when the sunlight hit it, tromped through the bushes and lumbered down the knoll toward the cave. Three steps later, the dark hole of the cave's entrance swallowed him.

We waited, our eyes fixed on the entrance. After a long period of time passed, the man came out carrying a large sack on each shoulder and left the way he'd come.

I waited until I couldn't hear any more human sounds and hurried down the mountain. I didn't think about how much noise I was making, until a twig snapped beneath my foot. The loud crack resonated through the trees. I stopped. Simon stopped.

"I hope they didn't hear that," I whispered.

Chapter 7

Two hours later, we stepped out of the woods into the hot sun, and Simon trotted toward the house. Judging by the angle of the sun, it must have been early afternoon, and my rumbling stomach reminded me of my half-eaten sandwich at the top of the mountain. I felt like someone had punched a hole in my toes and drained all my energy. Unlike my rambunctious companion, I passed the lake, ignoring the critters hovering near the water. I focused on the distance between me and the house until I noticed Rosa Leigh sitting in a chair on the deck.

Why is she outside in the hottest time of the day . . . slumped forward?

I ran to her.

She had her elbows on her knees, her face in her hands, and she was sobbing. Simon's front paws were on the bottom of her chair, and he was licking her arms and fingers.

My toe hooked on the bottom stair. I landed on all fours, crawled to my friend and hugged her tight. After what seems like an eternity, she stopped crying, and I handed her a crumpled tissue from my jeans.

Rosa Leigh looked at me through teary eyes and sighed a pitiful breath. "I'm so thankful you came when I asked." A tear trickled down from the corner of her eye. She blotted it and reached for my hand. "You always let everyone cry on your shoulder without asking questions. I appreciate that trait most." She brushed a wet spot on my blouse and motioned for me to sit.

"Sorry I soaked your shirt wet," she said and sighed another long sigh. "I have basal cell ductal cancer in both breasts. The left side has two large tumors, and the right has a small one." Rosa Leigh's next words caught in a sob, and she swallowed. "The cancer is fast-growing and aggressive. The doctor set up an appointment at an oncologist for next week." Her sobs began again. When the tears stopped, she said, "I told the doctor this shouldn't be happening to me. I've never missed a single mammogram." She blotted her eyes again. "Because of the fibroid disease in my breast, the x-rays show up white. The doctor said it's like looking for a polar bear in a snowstorm."

She pounded the chair with her fists. "I'm livid. There is a three-dimensional x-ray that would have found it, but the insurance doesn't pay for it. Therefore, no one mentioned it to me. I cannot believe the incompetence of the medical profession."

I took my friend's hand and cried with her. When no more water flowed, Rosa Leigh said, "The surgeon told me treatment is individualized and often there is no need to do mastectomies. The cancer doctor will give me a second opinion next week."

The question *What's his prognosis,* like a coiled Copperhead, struck at my core. But, I just couldn't ask.

Rosa Leigh stood. "You know what?"

"What?"

"I've always wanted Dolly Parton breasts." She held her breasts in her hands. "With the fibroid cysts in these here, they've always been sore. A new pair big as her with no pain," she said and giggled. "I'll be the Pied Piper of all the single men in Three Pines."

We laughed until tears streamed down both our cheeks. Mine were not happy ones. And I didn't think hers were, either.

Rosa Leigh opened the back door and walked inside. "I don't know about you, but I'm starved. And I don't intend to let this disease steal my joy." She motioned for me to follow. "I want to hear about your trip up the mountain, but first, you need to answer a question. Do you want to eat lunch here and dinner out? Or would you prefer having your bigger meal now—meaning restaurant?" She asked and winked.

"Let's go to Three Pines," I said. "I need to see Blake and have him come out here. Let me shower, and I'll tell you about our harrowing morning experience on the way to town. Did you ask Janene which she prefers?"

Rosa Leigh opened her bedroom door. "She told me at breakfast she was going to work all day. She plans to stop for a sandwich and take a walk when she needs a break. According to her, all this running around is interfering with her creative flow," my friend said and chuckled. "I'm going to freshen my makeup."

"And I need a shower and to change clothes." A flash of the logged area flitted through my memory as I opened the bathroom door." Oh, do you know that someone has logged trees recently?"

"Don't tell anyone," she whispered, "but I allowed one of my neighbors to cut wood for the winter. He lost his job and has three children. He helps me when I need something done and won't let me pay him. This is pay back."

"He stripped one area of everything but saplings."

"I don't need the trees," she said, shrugged and closed the door.

I stripped out of my sweaty clothes and walked to the shower.

* * *

Blake found us at Rosa Leigh's usual table at the back of Nettie's restaurant.

We ordered and talked pleasantries until the meal came. While he forked a bite of food, I told him about the incident on the mountain. When I was done, I took my phone from my purse and showed him the photos.

As he studied them, I scooted forward in my chair. "They definitely were not interested in the skull or the jar, and they're claiming the cave for storage," I said, waiting for Blake to comment. When he didn't, I continued, "It appears the first two men were leaving something in sacks. The third one picked them up. What do you suppose they're doing?"

Blake speared another piece of steak. As he chewed, a scowl deepened the crevice between his brows. He swallowed. "I don't have a clue at this point, but," he said, punctuating his words with his fork, "the two of you are not to go back up there unless I'm with you. Understand?"

Rosa Leigh sliced her grilled chicken breast. When she raised her head, her hazel eyes sparkled. She placed her forearms on the table. "I have no plans to hike up there, but what Ives discovered today intrigues me. This is the most exciting thing on Copperhead Ridge in years." She pointed a finger at the Sheriff. "And, Blake, I want to know why three strangers are trespassing on my mountain. Until last Sunday, I didn't know about the cave. How long have those men known? I want to know how they're using it, and I want the details as you know them."

I shifted on my chair and said, "And since I'm the one who discovered all of them the second time, I want to be in on the action. Rosa Leigh hired me to find the owner of the skull. I plan to go back there tomorrow morning and bring it home. If you don't want me to go alone, Sheriff, then be there ready to hike by 7:00 A.M."

He placed a hand on Rosa Leigh's shoulder. "Use whatever power you have over your employee to keep her away from the cave. Those men could be dangerous." He pinched the small part of his nose. "Correction! They *are* dangerous."

I breathed deep to squelch the anger rising like a fierce storm through my body. "For your information, Blake Sheets, I am doing exactly what my employer hired me to do."

"Still a fireball," Blake said and laughed his familiar deep sound. "I bet your husband had his hands full all those years."

"I'm not the shy, bookish eighteen-year-old you knew," I said, trying to sound forceful, but his blue gaze was quickly melting my aggressiveness. "My husband and I were compatible."

Rosa Leigh chuckled. "No one can dispute the evidence. They had seven children, Blake."

Using quick jagged cuts, I sawed at my chicken cordon bleu.

"Ives, if I'm not called out in the morning, I'll be there at 7:00 A.M.," Blake said, evidently choosing to ignore the fact she'd had seven children. "I need the skull. A young man went missing two years ago. It might belong to him."

Rosa Leigh sipped her coffee. "Those parents have searched these hills for two years. I wonder if I'd want it to be my dead son, or would I want it to be someone else to keep my hope alive?"

Blake's cell beeped, and he answered it. "Be there in fifteen minutes, twenty at most." He put it back into the holder on his belt, pushed his plate back and stood. "Ladies, I wish I didn't have to leave, but there's been an accident."

He smiled at me. "I'll see you at 7:00 A.M."

"I'll be ready," I said and then cut another chunk of chicken. "It's a shame you have to leave without finishing your meal."

Nettie appeared and swooped up his plate. "I'll box it for him and drop it off later." She leaned in and whispered in my ear, "Remember what I told you." And then she disappeared as fast as she came.

"What did she say to you?" Rosa Leigh asked.

I chewed the bite in my mouth, swallowed and took a drink of my lemon water. "She's acting crazy again. She says what you have me doing is dangerous."

Rosa Leigh laid her fork in her plate. "You better pay attention. The woman's visions," she flailed her hands in the air, "feelings, dreams, or whatever they are, might not come as often anymore, but she's still seldom wrong."

A sudden chill swept across the back of my neck. I focused on my food, but my voice quivered when I was finally able to speak, "Blake will be with me. Who's dumb enough to go up against the Sheriff?"

Chapter 8

Rosa Leigh and I spent the afternoon shopping in
Lexington. We returned home to find Janene on the dock,
lounging in an Adirondack chair. "I didn't think you'd ever
come home," she said. "I want to ride the jet ski, but I don't
want to do it without one of you here. I've never driven
one, and it's intimidating."

After Rosa Leigh showed her how to operate the
machine, Janene circled the lake, squealing like a teenager
asked out on her first date. As dusk settled into the valley,
the two of us chatted, and Simon snuggled Rosa Leigh's
leg without making a sound.

Janene tired out and locked the jet ski to the pier. The
three of us sauntered to the house, talking about the event
on the mountain. I expected Janene to order me to stop my
investigation. Instead, she remained calm, nodding her head
from time-to-time. "Be careful."

I put both hands in the air. "What can happen with the Sheriff there?"

She crossed the dining room to the hall. "This will add tension and suspense to my novel. Do either of you mind if I use bits and pieces?"

Rosa Leigh shrugged. "Not at all...if Ives doesn't mind."

I thought about it for a moment.

If she is using the episode as her plot or subplot or something, she'll stay out of my way. "Be my guest. I'm going to prepare Rosa Leigh and I a fake Reubin sandwich. Would you like one?"

"No, thank you. I'm not hungry. I'll have a protein bar or yogurt later," she said and disappeared down the hall.

I toasted four slices of whole wheat bread, placed rotisserie chicken slices, Swiss cheese and kraut on one slice of each sandwich and covered with the other pieces of toasted bread. I prepared one of my low-calorie recipes—sliced strawberries and whipped cream on chocolate graham crackers. While I prepared the food, Rosa Leigh gathered her yearbooks. Simon tagged along behind her.

As we ate, Rosa Leigh brought me up to date on our former classmates. Eventually, we retired to our separate rooms.

I tossed and turned, dozing occasionally, but waking around two. The comforter was in a ball. I straightened it and dozed off and on until daylight. When I dragged myself out of bed and shuffled to the bathroom, Simon followed me.

After a hot shower, I fed my buddy and fixed some pancakes—from a mix. By 7:00, I had a buttered stack ready for Blake. But, he didn't show. I gobbled my breakfast, stacked the plates in the dishwasher, grabbed my backpack and left—angrier than an antagonized bull in a fight.

When I reached the base of the mountain, I walked the tree-line until I found the broken and trampled shrubs I'd left as trail markers the day before and stepped beneath the canopy of leaves. Simon bounded across a patch of tall grass and raced up the hill.

Alone, I thought about Blake and what might be.

I have no family holding me in Florida. My children are scattered across the country.

I glanced around, trying to remain vigilant of my surroundings.

I love spending time with Rosa Leigh and getting reacquainted with my high school friends. And Kentucky is a beautiful state. It has lakes, caves, waterfalls, flat land and mountains untouched by humans. It's not far to large cultural centers, and some of the people are the most talented in the world. It has the rich, the poor . . . Goodness, I'm almost to the cave.

I walked through the steep and rocky, dry creek bed. A cliff with a gaping mouth stretched east a short distance. Farther up and to the left of several small sprigs, the oak and other bushes grew at the base of the giant tree that had shielded us from view. Stumbling, I crossed the broken shale, scrambled to the top of the cave and ran to where the skull laid yesterday.

But it wasn't there!

Frantic, I searched beneath the bushes, behind trees and underneath dead leaves. Disappointed, I collapsed on my knees. "I should have compromised the crime scene and taken it home yesterday."

Simon licked the tears off my cheek and sat beside me. "You're only doing this because you're thirsty," I said in a stern tone. His head dropped, and a few seconds later, when the dried leaves rustled in the shrubs, he chased a dark streak that darted out. "Come back here!"

Like always, he plunged headlong into the bushes, yelped and ran out whining. A pungent odor filled the air, and a skunk skittered away. Simon bounded toward me, his head bobbing up and down.

I thought about running, but I knew he'd outrun me. I couldn't let him rub against me. And I couldn't touch him. The smell of skunk would saturate my skin and my clothes. I stepped off into the creek bed at the mouth of the cave and yelled. Simon skidded to a stop. "Rosa Leigh is going to kill me, and you'll be banished to the porch tonight. Go home!" I pointed down the trail.

He whined and shook his head. He didn't like the skunk smell, either. After he disappeared over the mountain, I turned my thoughts back to my dilemma.

Maybe one of the men found the skull. Or someone else found this spot.

As I searched for footprints near the exit trail the men used the day before, a rock wobbled underneath me, my ankle turned and pain shot up my leg. I hobbled to the edge of the creek bank and leaned against it. When the pain subsided, I sat down to untie my shoe, but jumped to both feet when something large thrashed through the bushes toward me.

I froze.

The burly man with the mustache and deep booming voice appeared. "Hands on the back of your head and kneel."

The wrinkled bandana tied around his nose and mouth caved in and blew out with each word. He pushed a limb out of his way and stepped down. I recognized his cold brown eyes, the soiled white cotton t-shirt and raggedy blue jeans. He pulled a navy cap, with the Three Pines' Wildcat logo, lower and motioned with his .22 rifle for me to kneel.

I glanced at the ground and realized the rock would cut my sixty-two-year-old skin to pieces.

"Kneel, lady!"

"Surely you wouldn't make your mother kneel on rock."

"You're not my mother."

I weighed my odds...

A man with a gun against one terrified lady about to pee herself.

I stopped arguing and began to bend, but when a twig snapped behind me, I whirled. A second masked man was holding a 9mm on me.

A vivid scene from a mob movie where three men were made to kneel, their murderer shooting them in the back of the head, flashed before my eyes.

As I lowered to the ground, my knees collapsed. I hit the jagged rocks, and my shrill scream echoed through the trees.

The burly man stumbled towards me and stopped. "You're closer," he said to his partner. "Go down there and shut her up!"

When the skinny man jumped down the hill, the rocks underneath him cracked. He stepped towards me and raised his pistol above his head.

I rolled myself into a ball.

Mustache man screamed, "Don't hit her!"

He inched down the slope himself, loosening stones and debris. When he stood over me, he said, "I have a better idea. Stand up."

I tried, but my jelly legs wouldn't listen to my frightened brain.

He poked me in the back with the cold barrel of his rifle, and I struggled to my feet. He motioned the rifle toward the cave. I stumbled over the rocks towards the opening.

The wiry man stood at the entrance, facing me and Mustache. He raised a shaky hand to his temple and massaged. "What are we going to do with her?"

"Lose her," Mustache said. He nudged me in the back with his gun barrel.

I shivered.

"Wait a minute," the wiry one said. "She's wearing a back pack. She probably has a cell phone in it."

"It won't matter." Mustache man yanked at my bag.

I wiggled out of it.

He handed it to the short one. "Take out flashlights and weapons."

"I'm hiking," I said, irritated by his stupidity. "Who carries lights and guns on a hike?"

Mustache sniffed. "We do."

I shrugged. "Oh yeah."

"Step away from her," Mustache said.

I closed my eyes and prayed.

Chapter 9

I cringed and squeezed my eyes tight, waiting for the shot.

Will I feel anything? Or will it be in the back of my head and painless because it travels through my brain?

I eased my head around and opened my right eye a smidgen. Mustache was standing where I could see half of him, cool as an ice cube.

Wish I had a piece of ice right now. I'm parched.

He stepped closer.

My heart galloped, and I shut my eye. I didn't want to see him shoot me.

"March!" He ordered.

The gravel crunched. The cold barrel jabbed between my shoulders. I jumped.

"Move, Grandma!" He yelled.

Fiery anger boiled up, taking control of me. "Don't call me grandma. You're too old to be my grandson...and way too stupid."

He pointed the gun at my eyes and held the barrel close enough for me to feel the cold metal. "Who's the dumb one now? Hotfoot it, or I'll shoot your eyes out."

I stared into the rifle barrel, scared spitless and wobbled toward the opening in the mountain. A red cardinal landed on the limb of the oak, above where I'd seen the skull. It chirped. And higher up a hawk cawed and circled.

How can those birds act normal? This scene is insane.

The small guy entered the cave, and dread spread over me like a blanket of doom. I hate bats, and cold dark places remind me of coffins. I whispered a prayer.

Mustache pushed me.

As I took a step, the cold damp air chilled me, and the dank odor reminded me of the old cellar my family had years ago.

Using a butane lighter, the small guy lit a lantern, and the glow glistened off the walls surrounding us. A drop of water splashed in a puddle somewhere. Something scurried to my right, so I edged against the opposite wall, moisture soaking my sleeve.

I remembered a talk a tour guide gave at an Ohio cavern. He said there's a whole ecological system in caves, and some creatures cannot live in sunlight. I hadn't paid close attention to the information. And I wished I had. Who knows what critters were in here?

The squirrely guy held the lantern high above his head, and his eyes rolled upward.

I inspected the ceiling. No visible bats—yet.

We stepped over a large rock and splashed through a shallow puddle. The narrow passage became wider and wider, and we entered a large room-like area. We inched along the only way through. The room appeared to become narrower. I touched straw-like features forming from the ceiling. Droplets of water formed at the bottom of each one, and some were no larger than my pinkie. Others were fatter; their thickness more the size of my thumb.

The leader made a left into another channel, and I made a mental note to remember the turns. As we meandered this way and the other and passed through three or four more chambers, the upward grade taxed my weary calves. When we strolled into a larger area, stalactites and stalagmites formed columns from ceiling to floor. On one wall, a small stream flowed through a tiny hole near the ceiling. The water shimmered in the glow of the lantern as it rippled over the uneven rock to a pool in the floor. The stream trickled over and around other formations into a narrow stream and disappeared into the darkness.

Mustache nudged me against the cave wall. "Sit."

I did as he asked, and the cold moisture soaked the seat of my jeans. I shivered once more.

Mustache said, "Don't twitch a muscle." He turned to the other guy. "Hurry up and fill those two sacks." He fixed me with his frosty eyes. "This one probably made us miss our connection."

Squirrely guy shoved what appeared to be bottles of cold medicines in one bag. In the dim lighting, though, I couldn't be sure that's what it was. He stuffed small boxes in a second bag. As the last sack reached the halfway mark, my breath quickened.

I'm a dead woman.

Squirrely carried one of the filled sacks to Mustache. He threw it across his left shoulder. As Squirrely filled the second bag he asked, "We going to leave her untied?"

Mustache glowered at me. "Why not? With no light, she'll never make it out."

Squirrely pivoted my way. "I don't like thinking about her living to identify us later."

"She hasn't seen our faces, Nitwit," Mustache said. "I'm telling you, she'll never get out of here." He disappeared into the dark shadows.

His cohort skulked behind, and the glow of their lantern was quickly fading.

I examined the chamber view in what was left of their lantern's glow.

"How will I find my way out of here?"

Then blackness enveloped me.

Chapter 10

The men's voices echoed through the tunnel, fading as they walked, and as I called out, "Don't leave me here! I won't tell anyone I saw either of you. I won't tell them anything about what you're doing up here. Your secret is safe with me."

I listened.

Something rattled a small stone close to me.

A spider? I detest those creepy furry things. "Help! Please!"

Whatever was above me scurried away. A stone rolled over a ledge and landed near me. I patted the area where it dropped and touched pebbles and a large embedded stone. When a damp, soft critter darted across my hand, I jerked it away. Little, medium and big-sized feet scrambled, scuttled and dashed around the walls, ceiling and floor. Something monster-sized skittered across my outstretched leg. I screamed. Pandemonium set in.

Hugging my legs to my chest, I ducked my head inside my arms and made myself into as small a ball as I could. Crunched up, I couldn't breathe, though, so I raised my head. Using the wall, I pushed myself up and gulped precious air. When my lungs were full, my heart pumped slower, and I talked to God.

"Father," I whispered. "You know I've been terrified of the dark since I was little, and the raccoon crawled through my open bedroom window. I carry the scars the varmint made on my legs and hand. A nightlight burns in every room of my home. Please, please, please hear my prayer. Help me." And then, I sobbed until no more tears would come. I hiccupped. Swiping the water and snot off my face, I wiped it on my jeans.

My mind drifted. *I wonder how all those folks in Florida are doing? I need to check on the hurricane status. If I escape from here, I'll watch the news tonight.*

I shook my head. "Sorry, Lord. You know I have trouble focusing for very long. You know my thousands, maybe millions, of warts and moles. I'm undeserving of Your favor, but I'd sure like it. Please show me the way out of this hillside. Don't let it be my grave. Amen."

When I stopped praying, it was quiet. Water trickled into a puddle, or creek, or stream in front of me. I stretched out my hands and inched my feet forward. *The water exits somewhere. Otherwise, this cavern would be flooded. If, and it's a big if, I can follow it until it flows into another tributary, maybe I'll find the way out.*

Shuffling across the ground, I checked my footing each step, until I felt the front part of my foot not on a solid surface. I squatted and felt below my toes. There was an opening. I placed both hands on the ground, laid on my stomach and pushed my arm down until my fingers touched cold liquid. I reached across as far as I could, but I couldn't touch the other side.

Okay, how do I follow this without falling in? It might not be deep, but it could be. If I tumble in, I might not surface. I might go all the way to Antarctica, and I'll freeze to death before I'm rescued. So, how do I do this? If I lose my balance, I can't grab the wall behind me. It's too far away, and there are no sticks in here to use for support. The only thing I know for sure is to travel to my right, the direction we came and the way the men left.

Wait!

My brain cells fired up.

The water in here must be pure. There haven't been too many people in here to muck it up—unless those men polluted it. At least, I won't die of thirst.

I found the wall of the cave and placed one hand on it, wiggled my right foot all around, but nothing. I slid my foot around again. Nothing. Sidestepping two times the other way, I did the same using my left foot. Nothing. Inching further, my toes touched a furry mound.

I squealed.

Sounds of scurrying echoed through the cavern.

"Get used to the sound of me and my voice, critters. If you don't touch me, I won't hurt you. I want to be here less than you want me here."

Arms stretched in front of me, I shuffled my feet, making certain earth was beneath me. When I couldn't feel the ground, I stopped. There was a drop-off, and I knew I'd found the stream. I creeped along with my left toe on the edge of the embankment.

My balance was shaky, and I was disoriented in the abyss. I bent, touched the earth and sat. My head felt woozy, and I was suddenly exhausted and sleepy.

I should have drank water while I climbed. I think I'm dehydrated. At least the critters are quiet. I can't imagine living in total darkness. If I never see dark again, I'll be happy.

After a bit, I felt rested and decided to crawl. But it didn't take long before the excruciating pain in my knees travelled above and below them. Sitting on one hip, I placed my palms on the earth ahead of me and pulled my lower half to my hands. I travelled far enough that way to make my hip ache and then switched to the other one.

As I snailed along, I used my hand to check behind me for the stream. It was still there. By the time I went far enough to soak my clothes with sweat, my second hip was raw. I stretched my legs out in front. Thirsty and hungry and in so much pain, anger rolled up from my grumbling stomach.

If I see one of those men again, I'll shoot him. Or beat him over his hard head with the barrel of a gun. And if Simon dares to try to follow me again, I'll shoot him, too. Where is he when I need him most?

I laughed out loud. *Who am I kidding? I can't shoot a gun because I don't like the sound. I target practiced with my husband once, and my trigger finger swelled up like a cooked hotdog. It stayed sore for a month. To this day, I have pain in my middle knuckle.*

I placed my left toe at the edge of the stream and walked until I felt shaky. Sitting, I waited for the dizziness to disappear. When it didn't, I scooted back away from the water and curled into a ball.

I felt like I was floating near the ceiling.

Blake is below.

Simon's running ahead.

Was I hallucinating or were they really with me?

And then . . .

Chapter 11

The sun was shining through the fog at the top of the mountain. Strangely, there were two of me. One floated near the ceiling. Below that, a younger me was running with Rosa Leigh across a field covered with yellow dandelions.

I'll bring Momma here later, and she'll pick greens and fix them for supper. With this many, she'll make us gather enough to make wine. When I grow up, I'm never eating a dandelion again.

Rosa Leigh turned and called, "Last one to the berry patch is a rotten egg."

I chased after her, swinging a pail.

Then, Blake streaked past.

CLINK!

Startled, I jolt awake. Little feet scurry . . . maybe not so small. . . Don't care . . . Tired . . . Head's heavy.

"Ivesssss…," a voice echoed through the chambers of my grave. "Wake up."

I tried to open my eyes. They wouldn't work. I attempted to lift my head. I couldn't do that, either. At least, my shivering seemed to vibrate my eyeballs.

"Ivesssss…," the voice trilled. "It's Nettie. "Tell me where you are, and I'll come help. Or send someone else."

I tried to answer, but my tongue was too thick and dry. *Deep in the cave, Nettie.* I drifted into a restless sleep.

Simon's bark jarred me awake. He sounded so far away, barely audible. I tried to call him, but my voice came out in a mousy squeak. His yapping grew louder, and I heard Blake's voice. "We're coming, Ives. Call again."

"I'm here!" I said as loud as I could, but I wasn't sure if I was being heard. I kept repeating the phrase, until a ray of light swept across the ceiling and down the wall. I began to sob, and the next second, Simon's wet tongue licked my face.

As Blake squatted in front of me, he said, "Hi, sweet thing. Can you walk?"

In the glow of the light, he looked blurry through my tears. *Did he call me sweet thing? He called me that name the three years we dated.*

I tried to raise my head and reach my hand to him, but I was too weak. His strong, muscular arm worked beneath my body and lifted me to a sitting position. My head lobbed to the side. A cool plastic bottle touched my lips.

"Drink. You're probably dehydrated."

I sipped.

He pulled the water away for a few seconds and then put the bottle back for me to drink. I swallowed small amounts until I no longer was thirsty. He set it aside and waved a sandwich beneath my nose.

The aroma of my favorite sandwich filled my mouth with water.

He remembered after all these years to brown baloney edges and top it with a piece of sweet onion. I love you, Blake Sheets. If you ask me to marry you again, I will accept before you can back out. Did I think that? Or did I say it?

I bit into the sandwich and held the meat and bread in my mouth to savor the flavor. I attempted to eat, but my jaws were frozen. *How can someone be too tired to chew?*

Blake held the sandwich to my mouth. "Take another bite. You need nourishment."

He was seated beside me with his legs stretched out, and I was leaning against him. A propane lantern lit the chamber. I stuck out my tongue with half-chewed food to show him I still had a bite in my mouth. It plopped out onto my lap.

Blake lifted the bottle to my lips. "Drink some more water. Your mouth is dry. If you swallow right now, you'll choke."

I listened to his heartbeat. *Take me home with you. I'll bake you all kinds of desserts. You won't need those women you're seeing now. I'll take care of all your needs.*

"Take another bite of baloney."

When he lifted the sandwich, the aroma of spicy onion and baloney filled my nostrils. *I can't believe I need someone to feed me. I'm the one who visits the sick, cares for them and takes them where they need to go.*

I chomped on the bread and ripped away the layers. *I will chew this if it's the last thing I do.*

When I couldn't open my mouth anymore, he screwed the lid on the bottle, placed three-fourths of the sandwich back inside the baggie and shoved both into his pack. He lifted me to my feet, but my legs buckled, and he grabbed me.

"Okay . . . then," he whispered, his words strained. "I must admit, I'm not a muscleman, but I think if I carry you piggy-back like I used to when we were kids, I can still handle the lantern. Here, Simon. We need you to carry the backpack."

Blake strapped the satchel on top of Simon's back and fastened the buckles under his belly. Simon grinned. "Good Boy. You lead the way, big fellow."

Simon turned and walked in the direction they'd come.

Blake lifted me. "Wrap your arms around my neck," he told me and jostled me into position. We walked until his knees buckled. He leaned me against the damp wall and asked over his shoulder, "Remember when our class took the field trip to Carter Caves?"

I nodded.

He chuckled. "The four of us, Rosa Leigh, Lucas Butler, you and me. We almost completed the tour of Bat Cave without being caught. If Rosa Leigh hadn't been such a girl, such a drama queen back then, we would have made it." He laughed again. "Poor Lucas pulled her through on his jacket, until the passage narrowed, and we had to crawl. She bawled like a sick calf most of the way, and her clothes were filthy when we scrambled out, like she'd wallowed in a pig pen. Can't believe the teachers didn't miss the four of us until the students were loading the bus."

I giggled. "The four of us were always in trouble. What one didn't think of, the others would, but we were never mean or violent. We were stupid kids who didn't realize the dangers," I whispered. "Remember our huckleberry outing?"

He rolled his head back, and his wonderful, deep laughter echoed through the corridor. "We took a five-gallon bucket to the woods and filled it with fruit. On the way down the mountain, Lucas mentioned his mother had a cold pitcher of cream in the refrigerator. Poor Lucas. He got into so much trouble because we used his house to hang-out. To this day, I can't smell or eat a huckleberry."

"Me either."

"Ready?" He asked.

We began our trip out of the cave, me riding piggyback.

"Simon, lead the way," Blake said.

I'd seen men carry bodies piggyback in movies. But those bodies were dead. With every step, pain shot through my stomach to my back, reminding me I was very much alive.

Blake carried me until he needed to rest. I lost count of the times we stopped, but after a while, the air felt warmer and rays of daylight filtered into the tunnel. Finally, we stepped out of the cave into the dappled shadows.

"I'm going to lay you down . . .," he said and paused, taking a gulp of air, "...and roll you down the mountainside." His demeanor had hardened, not a smirk or a grin visible.

"I'll curl into a ball and roll down, if the need arises," I said, not sure if he was joking or not.

When he put me on the ground, Simon stretched out beside me. Blake pulled a hatchet from his belt and held it up for me to see. "You forget I was a boy scout, and I'm a hunter. This is not the first time I've rescued a person on this mountain. You're much prettier and lighter than the last one, though."

He strolled to the saplings at the edge of the tree line, chopped and stacked a pile of long poles, all about the size of my wrist. Next, he found a tree covered with a vine, cut the limber parts close to the ground and assembled a bed for me by tying the poles together with vines. He laid the contraption next to me, helped me onto it, and Simon led us down the mountainside.

"When you're home and rested, I'll have you check the mugshot data base. Those men are probably in the system." His voice vibrated with his steps. "And you'll fill me in on what happened up there."

I will?

Chapter 12

When Blake and I made it to Rosa Leigh's house, there was a handsome doctor waiting—one who had a beautiful smile, brown eyes, brown hair and soft hands. After he and Blake helped me off the improvised travois and into the house to bed, I said, "I didn't know doctors still make house calls."

"I don't, but Blake is my friend." He gave me a quick, Crest-white smile. "I was golfing with some out-of-town friends when he called me."

I struggled to sit up but decided against it and plopped back against the pillow.

"Leave it to Blake . . ..," I murmured, "...to ruin a perfect day." I gulped for air, but the hippopotamus that was apparently on my chest was blocking it.

Blake cleared his throat and left the room.

The doctor placed a pulsar thing-a-ma-jiggie on my finger and an ice-cold stethoscope against my chest. "I'm

Doctor Bell. Yes, Blake is known for disrupting people's days. Take a big breath for me."

I followed his instruction.

He placed the stethoscope in another spot. "Breathe deep and blow out."

Two more times he positioned the thing, and I took a deep breath and blew out.

"Are you married?" I asked, figuring I should probably get to know my doctor.

He unclamped the instrument from my finger. "Your oxygen level is good, but your heart rate is elevated. Let's check for a concussion and broken bones."

His fingers kneaded my head. "No lumps or cuts on the scalp. Did you fall?"

I rolled my eyes back in my head, thinking. "Don't know. Are you my and Blake's age?"

Dr. Bell took my left arm and checked front and back, laid it gently on the bed and did the same with the other one. "No cuts or abrasions."

"You're too young to be a doctor. I'm guessing you're younger than us?"

He scratched the side of his mouth. "Blake was my dad's best friend. I'm going to help you sit up because I need to examine your chest, ribs and back. If you feel pain during this exam, let me know."

He tapped my clavicle bones, pressed on my ribs and moved his fingers along the sides of my spine. "You can sit on the bed again." He knelt in front of me. "When we helped you into bed, I noticed both denim legs were torn through at the knee and right buttock, and the skin was bleeding on your thighs. It could lead to a serious infection if not treated. I need for you to remove your jeans, so I can clean and treat the areas."

I scooted closer to the edge of the bed. "I'm Ives. Don't you think we should be on a first name-basis before you ask me to remove my jeans?"

He sat in the rocker beside my bed. "If you prefer, I can call the EMT's and you can go to the emergency room." He paused for me to grasp his statement.

I stood, staggered back and fell forward.

Dr. Bell jumped from the chair and steadied me. He flashed a gorgeous smile and said, "Weak, are you? Place your hand on my shoulders."

I did as he asked and said, "You smell like a walk in the woods."

He lifted a brow. "Thanks . . . I think."

Attempting to unbutton my jeans with my left hand, which was a dumb idea, since I struggle with two hands due to my stiff fingers, I staggered back and forth. "You'll have to unfasten them," I said, smiling.

He grunted something inaudible, undid the button and unzipped my pants. "Can you take them off?"

My legs felt weak, but I pushed down my doggone pants. I pulled one leg free, but the other stuck on my shoe. I kicked, but it clung fast. Bending to pull it off, I shifted my weight to one foot and fell sideways. He caught me and stood me erect, and I huffed and puffed.

"Sit," he barked.

My knees gave way through the process. Bouncing onto the bed, the doctor grabbed me before I landed flat on my back on the floor. He took my right leg, untied my walking shoe, pulled it off and did the same on the left side. He pulled off my pants and put them on the rocker. Snidely he asked, "Can you turn over by yourself?"

"For a handsome guy like you, I can do anything you ask this half-naked woman to do."

"Then please do it," he said, obviously not amused by my antics.

As I rolled to my right side, pain sizzled through my thigh to the bone. I groaned and moaned as I finished the turn-over. Eventually, I was on my stomach, and I wished I could stay there until Christmas.

Dr. Bell cleared his throat and asked, "Are you ready?" I grunted.

Paper ripped. Something cold swiped my raw skin. I breathed in a deep breath and gritted my teeth. "Burn, burn," I said and breathed in and out fast, like a well-done Lamaze technique. "See if I take my clothes off for you again."

Another packet ripped open, then the cold, followed by searing pain. It zinged up and down my other hip. "Okay. I'm sorry. I won't tease you anymore."

He dabbed a cold liquid on each side. My hips were on fire, the pain level almost as high as having a baby.

He gathered the trash off the bed. "No more prodding and poking today. I'll make an appointment for you to see my associate, Dr. Teresa Moffett, next week at our office."

I burst out laughing. "Surely, you're not afraid of a sixty-two-year old lady, Doc."

He walked to the door, turned and said, "No, I'm not. I'm going to be out of the office. I'll send in Rosa Leigh to help you dress." And he disappeared down the hallway.

My friend bustled into the room babbling, "You almost caused me to have a heart attack, Ives Schnepe. Why did you go up there without Blake? What happened? And how did you end up in the cave?"

I let her jabber while she dressed me. When she finished slipping a night gown over my head, I curled up in a fetal position. "I'll answer . . . later." A blanket covered me, and I faded away.

Chapter 13

Loud voices woke me. I glanced around the strange bedroom, trying to acclimate myself. The room was spacious, large enough for me to set half my trailer in. There was an antique vanity at least six feet long against one wall. A tall oak wardrobe, one like my parents once owned, sat against another wall.

When a woman with a shrill voice cackled in the living room, I clambered out of bed, snatched my robe and staggered into the spinning hall. Leaning against the wall, I listened.

A gruff voice asked, "What happens when you let gas in the church?"

Ladies giggled and Rosa Leigh said, "Tell us. We haven't a clue."

"You sit in your own pew."

The women cackled.

The same scratchy, deep voice said, "Wait! I'll tell one more. What do the mice and rats call Jesus?"

There's low chatter while the women try to guess the answer.

"We don't know," Rosa Leigh said.

Sliding one bare foot in front of the other, I crept through the hallway until the speaker was visible. Mildred, a.k.a. Red, a nickname from grade school because she didn't like her name, placed her hands together in prayer form, bowed her head, and said, "Cheesus."

A bottled blond with dark roots waved her hands. "I have one."

Rosa Leigh stood. "This is the last one, or we'll be until midnight playing Hand and Foot."

Spike said, "I'll hurry. A husband and wife go shopping for groceries. The man stashes a can of peaches in his coat pocket. When they leave the store, the alarm goes off, and he's caught. Standing in the court room a few days later, the judge asked, "How many peaches were in the can you stole?"

The man scratched his head and said, "I don't know. They were sliced, and I didn't open the can. Maybe four."

The judge banged his gavel and said, "You will spend four days in jail for shoplifting, one for each peach you took."

He pounded the stand again for emphasis.

The wife stood and raised her hand. "Your Honor, he took a can of peas last week."

Laughter filled the room, and Rosa Leigh waved them to the card tables. Still holding the wall, I pushed one foot and then the other, until the support of the wall was behind me. Running to the sofa, my bare feet smacked against the cool wood. Someone grabbed my arm. Their nails clawed my skin, and I squealed.

"My goodness, Ives," Rosa Leigh said. "Why didn't you ask for help?" She steadied me to a chair.

"Thought I could do it myself."

An unknown voice said, "You were always in trouble doing things your way."

Squinting, I studied her face. "If it isn't Jersey Donovan. When did you lower your tight—"

A hand clamped over my mouth, and the scent of the watermelon hand soap from the kitchen filled my nose. Rosa Leigh whispered into my ear in a no-nonsense voice, "None of your old labels. We are adults now, and you are a professional. Act like one." She uncovered my mouth and directed her conversation away from me and to the others, "Ladies, go ahead and shuffle the decks while I seat my friend."

I looked up at her and said, "All of you have had time to settle your differences. I still remember Jersey acting like we were dog doo on her shoe, and now, she's part of the group. Forgive me if I see her as the tight—"

Rosa Leigh's hand sealed my lips again and my nose. I clawed her fingers away. "I hope you got a handful of snot."

Rosa Leigh straightened from her hovering position, leaving behind the light fragrance of gardenia. "You're the Sunday morning church goer. You've heard of forgiveness, haven't you?"

Mumbling, I asked, "Do I look like Christ? I can't forget all the nasty, mean things."

Rosa Leigh scratched above one eyelid. "Jersey's changed over the years, and she's become a charitable, kind person. She's the first to arrive with food when one of us is sick."

I leaned forward in my chair, grabbed her blouse and pulled her down. "And the first to make a snarky remark about how I find trouble all the time. A snake sheds it skin every year, but it's still a snake."

Rosa Leigh huffed. "Do you feel up to playing cards?"

I hitched my head toward the two tables. "I'll play if I'm not *her* partner." I placed both hands on the chair's arm, pushed my bottom halfway up off the chair and dropped. Rosa Leigh helped me to the table.

Red dealt the cards to assign partners, her sterling silver bracelet tingling against the table.

When she saw I would be her partner, Maggie Winchester sighed. "I hope you know the game Hand and Foot."

"I do, but I haven't played it in years."

When I had my first Meld with a fifty-point joker and two tens, her lack of charm stung me. "It's better if you keep the joker and the twos until we are on the board. You may need the wild cards later. When I play my hand, you'll see why."

I scrunched my face. Nettie must have sensed my irritation because she bumped my knee. I glanced at her out of the corner of my eye, and she smiled. I wanted to say something nasty to Maggie, but I didn't, for Rosa Leigh's sake. *I am a professional, and I'll bite my tongue.*

The other players took their turns, and when it reached my partner, she laid down seven tens.

Maggie said, "You ruined a red book by using your joker. We have three hundred points instead of five hundred for all tens."

My skin prickled. "Why didn't you tell me you had seven tens?"

Maggie's brow arched.

Gritting my teeth, I replied, "Because you are not allowed to talk across the table, that's why. And surprise! I didn't wear my magic glasses. So, I can't see what you're holding."

It rankled her even more when we finished low score on the first round.

As we shuffled the cards, Rosa Leigh announced, "There's a new play at the Comedy Theater in Columbus. Who wants to go next month? We can eat dinner, find a hotel and see the show."

Nettie finished counting the foot and passed it to Red. "I'd love to go, if my assistant manager can run the restaurant for me. I'll let you know next week."

"Who else?" Rosa Leigh asked.

Janene spoke up. "I need a break. I'd love to go and take my mind off my novel." She turned to Elizabeth Reynolds. "Are you retired?"

Elizabeth scowled at Janene. "How old do you think I am?"

Embarrassed, Janene said, "No, no. I was trying to be friendly. I didn't mean you look old. What do you do?"

"Why do you ask? Are you planning to include the information in your book?" Elizabeth took a card from one place in her holder and put it in another spot. She wrinkled her nose and stared at Janene. "Some people can't tolerate nosy strangers."

Jersey Donovan frowned and said, "She works at the post office."

Janene took a deep breath and smiled at Elizabeth. "I wasn't trying to be nosy. I want to get acquainted with you ladies." Janene shifted in her chair and gazed at me. Whispering, she asked, "Why don't they want me asking questions?"

Red chuckled and smiled at Janene. "Don't let her gruffness scare you. She's the nosiest old biddy around here. I want to know what happened to Ives. Spill, Woman."

"There's nothing much to tell, but I can't talk and concentrate on the card game. I'll tell you during dessert. I would like for someone to tell me why there is a ruckus about not asking questions, though. When I left here, everyone knew everyone else's business, and everyone helped their neighbors."

Red pushed the card container to the next person and said, "Every town changes a lot in forty years. It's called progress, except in this area, it's called migration. It began when we all graduated. First, the garment factory closed and sent all the work to Mexico. Then the shoe factory shut down. The steel mill in Ashland couldn't hire all the people who were laid off. And small business after business closed, until people had to search for work."

"But there are all these new houses going up. How are the folks paying for them, and where are they coming from?"

Rosa Leigh chimed in. "Many of the new homeowners are commuting to Columbus, Cincinnati or Lexington. They're not friendly, and a few of them are known drug dealers. Since our teenager came up missing, folks are scared."

"The theater closed when the jobs left," Nettie said. "We have to drive to Morehead or Ashland to see a movie or go bowling. Jess kept the pool room and café open until last year. His place became a hangout for the young people after Phillips' drive-in closed. It's no wonder the kids cause trouble around here. And a lot have turned to alcohol and drugs."

I handed my player cards to Maggie and said, "The local boy killed two years ago and the pill mill traffic from here to Florida made the news in my area. The FBI had surveillance on the pain clinics and discovered a steady stream of cars from Kentucky visiting the doctors and leaving the state the same day. A lot of the kids from this state were arrested, and the clinics were shut down. Supposedly, the trafficking between the two states stopped, but who knows? The news media also mentioned the killing while they were reporting."

Maggie interrupted as if she could care less about what we were discussing, "We need two red and two black books, Ives. Why don't you hold your wild cards or play the jokers and twos on a hand with six cards?"

Nettie continued the former conversation, "The boy was tortured, and he was only nineteen." She clicked her tongue twice. "His best friend disappeared a month later. The rumor mill said the two sold drugs and spent the money. A lot of people in these parts think the missing boy was murdered because his car was left with the doors open, lights on and blood on the passenger seat. But the sheriff before Blake said until a body was found, he couldn't do anything. The no-account law man didn't bother to ask for outside help. Blake was his deputy and ran for the office in the Fall and won."

"I can't stop myself," I said and soldiered on with my questions. "Did you see signs about either boy's death, Nettie?"

She shook her head. "No, thank God. And I'm glad I didn't. I have enough nightmares."

"Does Blake know how the drugs are coming in?" I asked.

Nettie shrugged. "If he does, he's not telling the public."

Maggie stiffened her back. "That man is the best sheriff we've had in years. He knows everything going on in this area. When he gathers all the evidence, he'll act."

I smiled. "Maggie Winchester, you said something complimentary about somebody. I'm impressed."

A smirk formed on her lips. "I praise people who deserve it."

As the women counted their scores, Rosa Leigh excused herself. "I'll turn on the coffeemaker." She walked to the kitchen and when she returned, she whispered into my ear, "Blake wants me to bring you by his office in the morning. We'll go before my doctor's appointment. He was furious with you earlier. You better hope he calms down."

Reminded that Rosa Leigh would be told her cancer treatment plan tomorrow and hearing that Blake would chew me out made my heart race.

Out of the blue, Red asked, "What's the latest news about the hurricane?"

"I've been in a cave. I don't know," I quipped.

She turned to Janene who sighed and said, "It's changed directions about three times, but as of the six o'clock news, it came ashore in Key West as a Category 5. It's expected to lose power as it travels over land. Hopefully, by the time it reaches the Bradenton and Palmetto area, it will be a tropical storm."

Red combed her fingers through her hair. "The video of the storm looked terrifying as it passed through the Caribbean and the Keys. Those poor folks will be digging out a long time."

I rose and pushed my chair away from the table. "I hope you're serving something besides dessert, Rosa Leigh. I'm starved."

Maggie skittered past me as if I were standing still. She picked up a napkin, silverware and a plate. "We serve only dessert on card night. Everyone eats dinner at home."

I followed Maggie's example and gathered utensils. "Well, la-de-da. I bake sweets, but I don't eat them often.

They cause you to have diabetes, and diabetes causes you to have a stroke or a heart attack. I am going to fry a hunk of Kentucky Border bologna and top it with a slice of sweet onion."

"Don't dirty up Rosa Leigh's kitchen this time of night," Maggie ordered.

I opened the refrigerator, took out the bologna and turned to the cabinet to pull out a pan. "You have clean-up duty, Maggie. So, no worries. I know you'll leave the kitchen spotless."

She marched to the table with an angel food cake, topped with strawberries and whipped cream. "The hostess cleans up."

I slapped a thick slice of meat into the hot skillet. It sizzled, and the aroma of the frying bologna caused my mouth to water. "Rosa Leigh hosts cards every week. It's time you ladies pitch in and help with clean up." I turned and pointed the spatula at Miss Maggie Snarky. "Better still, *you* should host the party next week."

Maggie's brows narrowed. "Rosa Leigh's the only one with a housekeeper, and she doesn't mind."

"Time changes things, right?" I said, narrowing my brows to match Maggie's.

Chapter 14

The next morning, I was as jumpy as a drop of water in a hot skillet when Rosa Leigh and I entered the Sheriff's Office at 8:30 A.M.

The aroma of coffee filled the air. I glanced around until I spotted the pot, rushed to it and poured a steaming cup. A squeak resonated in the room, and I knew what it meant. There were only two doors, one to the outside and one leading into Blake's office. I didn't turn around. He could talk to my back.

"I hope you can say what this hard-headed woman needs to hear in a half hour," Rosa Leigh said. "We do not have more time."

Blake's reflection was in a window. He was holding the doorknob. "This won't take long. Come into my office, Ives."

I turned, walked towards him with a cup of coffee in one hand and my other palm raised. As I entered his office, I said, "It was your fault. You didn't show up to go with me."

His cherry-wood desk was immaculate. There wasn't a folder or a piece of paper on it. Toward the front were two holders, one with his business cards and another with pens. Black metal file cabinets sat against the wall behind his desk. Two plush barrel chairs with wine-colored cushions faced his desk, and a padded cherry-wood ladder-back chair sat beside each barrel chair. The pale-yellow walls were bare, and the wood floor groaned with each step.

I glimpsed into his eyes for the first time. "Did you make the furniture?"

He motioned towards the seats, waited until I sat and stood next to my chair. "No."

I wanted to defend my actions, but I knew there was no excuse. I was stupid for going up there with only Simon. So, instead, I laced my fingers, placed my hands on my lap and waited for him to explode.

"If you do something this dumb again, I will arrest you for tampering with evidence. You will spend time in jail, until you have a hearing before a judge. I have enough crazy teenagers demonstrating risky behavior. I won't tolerate someone your age acting like them," he said and waited.

I rose from my chair and stood toe-to-toe with him. His fresh woodsy smell brought back so many memories. "I can't believe this. During high school, I fit beneath your chin. I've actually shrunk."

A smile spread across his lips. "I'm not kidding, Ives," he said. "What was your father's favorite expression when you were growing up? 'I say what I mean, and I mean what I say.' You believed him because he followed through on his word. Those men could have killed you instead of leaving you to die in the cave. You don't have the training to deal with this kind of criminal behavior. I mean what I say."

I tiptoed and kissed his cheek. "Thank you for caring." I strolled to the door and opened it. "I'm a private investigator and know what I'm doing."

He didn't need to know my training was nothing more than dealing with delinquent children. Some were meaner than a threatened rattler, though, and just as deadly.

I hurried through the outer office, waved for Rosa Leigh, and the two of us left.

As we exited Three Pines, traffic was heavy on the two-lane highway. We wound around mountains, through valleys, up hills and past small villages surrounded by fields of ripe corn and tobacco. At the Ohio River, a fishy smell mingled with the diesel from the semi in front of us.

We crossed the Portsmouth Bridge, travelled through side streets and made our way to the four-lane leading north. Two hours later, we were letting a valet park our car at the Mid-Ohio Oncology Office in Columbus.

I followed Rosa Leigh into the building. She nodded towards an office on her left. "There's where I will have radiation, if I need it." She walked a few more steps, punched the button, and the elevator doors opened. We stepped into the musty smelling space. She pushed the number two button, and we traveled to the second floor. My edginess was near panic mode, but I tried to hide it.

Rosa Leigh signed in at the reception desk. A lady clicked the computer keys, searched through a box to her left and pulled out a plastic sleeve. "Full name and date of birth, please."

My friend gave the receptionist the information, and a red paper band was fastened around her wrist. "Someone will come out and get you in a few minutes."

Rosa Leigh and I had a seat, but neither of us talked. Others chit chatted and laughed like this was a normal day. Soon, a nurse in purple scrubs opened the door and called Rosa Leigh's name. She took my hand, and we walked through the door.

A stringent odor swept past my face and made me shutter.

The nurse told Rosa Leigh to be seated. Four vials of blood later, she said, "Follow me."

We trailed her, like robots.

"Step on the scales."

Rosa Leigh followed her directions. Ms. Purple jotted her weight on a form and motioned us to follow her again. Once in an examining room, Rosa Leigh's blood pressure and pulse were taken, and the nurse entered the information into a computer. "The doctor will be in shortly," she said, and the door closed behind her.

We sat there, as if waiting for a judge to hand down a verdict. There was a knock. The door opened, and a short, thin man with dark brown skin and dark hair entered.

"I'm Doctor Kormanche." He wheeled a computer chair in front of Rosa Leigh and sat knee-to-knee with her. "I've studied your case. Your right side has a minute lump. We can do a lumpectomy. On your left breast, I recommend you have a mastectomy. There are three cancerous masses, and it has metastasized to the lymph nodes. We won't know how many nodes are cancerous until the surgeon operates. There are two more lumps in the center of your chest. The team decided it wasn't worth the risk of you getting a serious infection to open your chest to do a biopsy on those. Consequently, we don't know if those are cancerous. You are in Stage 3, if those two are not malignant, and Stage 4 if they are." He paused and patted her on one knee.

Rosa Leigh took a deep breath and blew it out.

And so did I.

He continued, "You'll need to call the surgeon and let the office set up the procedure. The sooner the better. After a six-week recovery period, you will return to me. You'll receive four chemo treatments. After they're completed, you'll have a rest period of a month and then receive radiation. For your kind of cancer, basal ductal, it usually means thirty-three treatments. You'll rest another month, and then I'll start your third stage of treatment. An over-abundance of hormones is the cause of this type of breast cancer, and the hormone blocker will suppress them. You'll take the pill each day for five years." He swiped his hands across each other. "You may have to take it ten years. Some take it seventeen, while others take the pill the rest of their life. We'll see you for check-ups to make certain the cancer doesn't return. Do you have any questions?"

Rosa Leigh took another deep breath and exhaled slowly before speaking, "What happens if I choose to do nothing?"

Dr. Kormanche shook his head, slowly. "You have a very aggressive cancer. It will spread, and it can be excruciatingly painful. With treatment, we have a good chance of eradicating it."

He waited for a response.

But Rosa Leigh was silent.

"We know a lot about your cancer because it is the most prevalent among women. The success rate is higher than it was even ten years ago. We've made great strides in the last decade," he said, stood up and pushed his chair back to the desk unit. "Do you have any more questions?"

Without hesitation, Rosa Leigh said, "I do the monthly exams and the annual mammogram with doctor follow-up. With the technology and advances, why wasn't my cancer found?"

"You have fibroid cysts of the breast. The x-ray shows as a static gray and white screen, and finding the malignant tumors is like searching for a polar bear in a snowstorm." Dr. Kormanche sighed a long breath and continued, "You needed a diagnostic breast x-ray, or a 3-D, to see the whole area."

"Why didn't the doctors tell me this?"

He took one of Rosa Leigh's hands. "Physicians need to do a better job of educating women in the breast cancer options. Most doctors are specialized in specific areas, and a family practitioner might not have known. But you are now in the hands of a knowledgeable team who are going to take excellent care of you. Call and schedule an appointment to see me the day the surgeon releases you."

He helped her stand, guided her to the door, and I followed.

As we walked the long hallway, my friend squeezed my hand. We rode the elevator down and waited for the car. Neither of us talked on the entire two-hour drive.

When we arrived home, Rosa Leigh told me to pull her car into the garage, something she didn't do unless she was home for the evening. She tossed her keys in the dish on the stand in the foyer, opened the closet door and hung up her purse, then walked down the hall to her bedroom.

It was two-thirty in the afternoon, and we hadn't eaten since breakfast. Ten minutes passed, and she entered the kitchen wearing a light, long-sleeved blouse and long pants.

"I'll have a sandwich ready in a minute," I said.

She opened the door, stepped out onto the deck and said, "I'm not hungry." She eased the door closed and disappeared.

I finished making a sandwich, fixed myself a glass of water with lemon and sat at the kitchen island.

The uncertainty of life smacked me in the face, specifically concerning Rosa Leigh. I chewed and chewed the first bite and suddenly felt an urgency to Facetime my seven children. Finding them all well and going about their usual routines, I placed my plate in the dishwasher, grabbed a bottle of water from the fridge and went in search of my friend.

She was behind the pool house in her vegetable garden, between rows, pulling up dried, withered plants. Simon was stretched out in the dirt near her.

When I handed her a bottle of cold water, I startled her.

"Goodness me," she said. She gulped the liquid and handed the bottle back, half-empty. "Thank you. Working in the soil is therapeutic."

"Why don't you let your gardener do this?"

She jabbed her shovel into the dirt. "He doesn't need the therapy," she said and smiled then tossed a dead plant into a nearby wheelbarrow.

"But you don't even use the vegetables, do you? You eat out all the time."

She dug beneath another specimen. "I take them to Nettie." She stopped working and said in a steely voice, "Don't go blabbing that, or she will be embarrassed. No one knows. I run them by her house after dark, or she comes by after work. Like the two of us, she's not as young as she used to be. Between her plot and mine, she is able to make a little profit at the restaurant."

I kneeled next to her. "Why not give her money? You said you will never spend all you have."

She chopped at the dirt. "Our friend has a lot of pride and would consider it as charity. This way, I tell her I have too many vegetables and ask her to take them to keep them from spoiling. I take some to church people, too." Rosa Leigh stabbed at the ground. "I swore when I grew up, I'd never want or need anything. And now?" Her voice cracked.

I dug around the root of a dead plant with a claw-like tool from her basket. "You've done well."

Tears spilled from her eyes. "Cole Adams rescued me. He built my confidence and made me who I am today. I'd give every dime to have him back and hear him tell me how beautiful I am." She swiped the tears off her cheek and left a black streak of dirt where they'd once been.

"God punished me for my wild streak by giving my first love cancer," she said and swallowed a sob. "Bob and I were happy, and he died after five years. It wasn't enough time. What did I do then? Crazy with grief, I grabbed the first nut case I found and married him. I should have killed David Free and his bimbo when I caught them in my bed."

Rosa Leigh rubbed the back of her gloved hand beneath her nose. "Adam Cole didn't care about my past." She pulled up the tail of her shirt and blew her nose.

"Neither do I, nor any of the people who love you, Rosa Leigh. And God didn't punish you. He only does good for His people. You made some bad choices along the way, but He's waiting for you to ask for His help. We all are waiting for you to tell us how we can help."

"A God who loves me wouldn't let all this happen," Rosa Leigh said, her voice rising to a shrill screech.

I realized I was in over my head, but I continued, "I don't know why bad things happen, and yes, God can stop them. I don't know why he doesn't. I asked Him why he took Jadan, when we were ready to retire and enjoy life." I sighed and then let out a bittersweet laugh. "God didn't answer. For a long time, I was angry with Him. I'm far from perfect. Every Christian is, but I know one thing today that I didn't back when I was bitter. God will be there to see you through the hard times. He can't leave us because the Bible says he won't."

Rosa Leigh dabbed her wet face with her dirty shirt tail. "I don't care about the old skull. You stop hunting it. I called you here because I need you. I don't want to go through this alone." She swatted my arm. "Understood? Stop looking."

She placed her shovel in her basket, pulled off her gloves and tossed them in. "I'm having a double mastectomy. I don't want to worry about the cancer returning. If there's no breast, the disease can't come back." As she struggled to her feet, tears welled up in her eyes again. "I don't want to lose my hair."

Sobbing, I stood and hugged her tight.

I can't stop the cancer, nor the needed treatment, but I can find the skull.

And I will, if it's the last thing I do.

Chapter 15

After Rosa Leigh and I went inside, I fried bologna and fixed a sandwich the way we loved it, browned on the edges and a sliver of Vidalia onion. I placed it on the island with a glass of skim milk, the only kind in the house.

She came out of her room, showered and smelling of her cherry blossom body soap. She didn't do her makeup—a sure sign she was worrying more than she was letting on.

As she slid onto the stool, I asked, "Have you called your son and told him yet?"

She placed her elbows on the counter, laced her fingers and tapped her lips. Tears streamed down her cheeks once more. "I'm waiting until I can tell him without crying." She fumbled in her pocket for a tissue.

I snatched a napkin from the holder on the counter behind me, stuffed it in her hand and said, "He's a grown man. At forty-one-years-old, he's seen life at its worst. He didn't live unscathed. In all my visits, his low-life father,

David Free, never acknowledged him. Why do you think he spent summers with my family? After you eat your lunch, call him. He'll never forgive you if you keep this from him."

She nodded and looked around the room, probably for her cell.

I placed my hand on hers. "Eat first. You probably left your phone in your room. I'll go look."

My knees were stiff from all the bending I'd done lately, but I limped to her room and back with her phone. "Look." I pointed to the French door. "You can't come in until I bath you, Simon," I said and turned back to face my friend. "He knows there's something wrong. Dogs are intuitive about those things. I had a friend who was a diabetic. She went into a coma, and her little dog woke her daughter who saved her mother's life. Did you see how Simon rested his head on his legs in the garden? His eyes never left your face. He's grieving, too."

She looked at me through eyes shimmering with tears. "Why do I have this mind-numbing and heavy feeling of grief in my chest? I'm not dying."

I shrugged. Some friend I am. I was creating more confusion for her. "Aren't you sad because you have the disease? I would be. And aren't you wondering what your life will be like without your breasts? Or if you'll feel healthy again? Don't you dread the first treatment? Not knowing is what's mind-numbing, Rosa Leigh. Yes, you feel grief, and you are entitled to experience it."

She swiveled her bar stool around and looked at Simon. "He's been a good friend since Cole died. He makes me feel safe at night." She went to the door, opened it and knelt to hug Simon. He placed his snout on her shoulder.

Rosa Leigh looked up at me. "Will you take him for his evening walk now so he can have a bath? He can't come in with dirt in his fur." She stroked his back. "You can come inside after your walk and a bath."

He cocked his head as if he understood.

I reached for his leash and snapped it onto his collar.

Rosa Leigh stood and said, "I'll call Mark later. I don't want to break the news to him on his job."

I nodded, gave Simon a little tug, and he followed me, glancing back at Rosa Leigh. I was hoping he wouldn't drive me berserk trying to chase cars as we headed to the old cemetery.

The trees edging the road cast long shadows across the gravel, indicating early evening. Two blue jays chased each other, chirping and squawking. High over the trees on the opposite side of the road, buzzards soared round and round. A few wispy clouds scudded across the sky above them.

Simon turned to look behind us, and I glanced back to see what he was interested in.

A large cloud of dust rose in the distance. At first, it was a speck, but it grew larger. Stones crunched and an occasional ping echoed through the air as gravel did when it hit metal. A red, four-wheel drive whizzed past. A dust cloud engulfed us, and I quickly closed my eyes and mouth.

When I opened them, Simon's sad eyes were fixed on mine. He didn't attempt to chase the vehicle. My heart broke. I bowed, hugged him and cried into his fur.

I don't know how long I cried, but Simon remained still. When my tears stopped, I took a tissue from my pocket and blotted the puddle of water from his coat. He turned his head far enough to gaze into my eyes and whimpered. I wanted him to howl at the top of his lungs. And maybe he would before this was over. We finally trudged on.

When we reached the cemetery gate at the bottom of the knoll, Ms. Overstreet was leaning against a tall gravestone, holding her head in both hands. Simon and I ran to her.

When she heard us, she glanced up and said, "Oh child, you are the answer to my prayer. A sudden weak spell came over me, and I nearly fainted. Will you take me home?"

I nodded, placed one of her arms around my neck and wrapped my other arm around her waist. We inched down the hill.

"He's a beautiful Golden Retriever. Ms. Adams brings him by on her walks sometimes. She brings a basket of vegetables from her garden in the summer. Nice neighbor, wonderful woman," Mertle said, her words coming in spurts.

I stopped often so she could rest, and so, our walk down the hill took a long time to reach the road. Since I wasn't planning to go for such a strenuous hike, I hadn't brought water, and I could tell by her speech that her mouth was dry. "I think you better save your breath and not talk."

She nodded.

I didn't check my phone, but it must have taken us ten minutes, or longer, to make it around the pond to the bench. Her legs were weak, and she dropped onto it as if her life depended on it. After she settled herself, she jerked her chin toward Simon. "Why isn't he swimming? He's sitting. Is he sick?"

I stroked his head, not sure what to say. "He must be concerned about you."

Satisfied with my answer, she told me the same history about the cemetery and the pond she'd mentioned the first time we met. After she rested about five minutes, we struggled across the grassy area to the woods.

The trampled path was narrow, and branches scratched my face, bringing tears, as I walked on with one arm around Ms. Overstreet's waist and the other holding her arm. The trees grew thicker, and the sun disappeared as we walked deeper.

"At one time, a bobcat was spotted in these very woods," she said. "Men searched for it, but never found it to kill it."

I hitched her arm a little tighter around my neck. "How long ago was this sighting?"

She was silent a few seconds. "Can't rightly say. Old people's memories aren't so good."

I inclined my head toward Simon. "He can handle a bobcat. But why would you be out here if there are dangerous animals around?" I shivered.

The tall grass lining the trail brushed my ankles, and I studied the ground in front of my feet. "Simon's smell is nine times more powerful than ours. We'll be okay."

"What about copperheads?" She asked.

I wanted to tape her mouth shut, but I didn't have the supplies. Who knew walking with Mertle would be more terrifying than the cave? "Dogs' hearing is nine times greater than ours. Simon will alert us."

She pointed forward. "The house is ahead," she said, panting faster than Simon.

The leaves rustled overhead, and I glanced up. A red squirrel jumped from one branch to another and chittered at us. I pressed onward. Soon, sunlight streamed through the gaps in the leaves. I tried to hasten my steps, but Ms. Overstreet was limp, almost total dead weight now. Her breathing was even more shallow than when we'd started out. I half dragged her through the last yards. As soon as I stepped into her backyard, I began yelling for help.

No one came. I trudged the last few steps to the screened porch. Thankfully, the door was unlocked. I don't know how, but I managed to help her up the two steps and into the main house. I reached a kitchen chair, yanked it out and let her drop into it.

"Hello!" I called out.

No one answered. There were muted voices in the next room, and so I hurried through the door. It was the television.

"Hello. Is anyone here?"

No answer.

A light blanket was turned back on the sofa, and a brown recliner had a scrunched, toss pillow against the back. There was no coffee table. On one end table, there were several medicine bottles, and the other end table was covered with magazines.

I walked to the front door and turned the knob. It was locked. After I looked through the rectangular glass in the middle of the door and saw no car in the driveway, I hurried back to the kitchen.

Ms. Overstreet's head was leaning forward, her chin resting on her chest. I returned with a pint jar filled with tap water. When I raised her head and touched the glass to her lips, she sipped.

I tore a paper towel from a roll above the toaster, wet it and cooled her forehead. Then, I gave her more water. I kept rotating the two until she rallied enough to walk to the sofa. Once she was settled, I asked, "Do you need medicine or food?"

She shook her head.

"Where's your daughter?"

"At work. She comes home around 5:30," she said, so weak her voice was nothing more than a low whisper.

"You're here alone all day?"

Her head plopped back against a pillow. "I'm not an invalid."

I checked the time on my phone. "She should be here any minute."

I realized Simon wasn't in the room and found him sitting where I dropped the leash. "Good boy."

Returning to the kitchen, I found an aluminum pie tin, filled it with water and carried it to him. He lapped it up fast. I give him more, and while he was drinking, I glanced around the porch.

The back wall was lined with three, old, matching bookcases. Baskets filled with folk art paintings and pottery vases splotched with faded colors sat on the top shelf.

This must be someone's painting studio.

I scanned the other shelves and recoiled. On the bottom one, tucked behind a large vase, was the skull!

Ms. Overstreet's voice jarred me, and I rushed to her.

"Where were you?" She asked, resting on one elbow. "You'll have to leave. If my daughter knows I walked to the cemetery and couldn't make it back by myself, she'll put me in a nursing home." Her eyes pleaded with me. "Please."

Gravel crunched out front. I hurried from the room, glancing back at the skull to make sure I wasn't imagining things.

If I take it, it will be stealing, and Blake will be obligated to file charges against me.

I ran out the back door, holding Simon's leash. We reached the woods, and I stopped. A car door slammed. Simon and I raced deeper into the trees and ran all the way to Rosa Leigh's front yard.

I grabbed my cell and placed a call...

Chapter 16

Blake didn't answer my call, so I left him a message.

Simon and I entered Rosa Leigh's house a lot faster than when we had left, huffing and, in his case, panting. He looked over his shoulder at me.

"Are you thirsty? I am," I said, filling his water dish and setting it by the door and then gulping a glass myself.

The place was quiet, so I called out, "Where is everyone?"

When no one answered, Simon and I searched for them.

Rosa Leigh was in her bed with a blanket over her ears. She jerked and whimpered.

Must be having a nightmare.

Simon laid on the floor beside her bed and rested his snout on his front legs. When I tiptoed to the mother-in-law quarters to see what Janene was doing, he didn't follow. When she didn't answer my knock, I opened the door and called her name. Still no answer.

The cherry desk was in front of a large window overlooking the lake. Her laptop was open but turned off. Papers, spiral notebooks and composition booklets lay at the side of the PC. Yellow, lavender, green, blue, and florescent orange Post-It notes lined the other side.

I glanced out the window. There she was, floating in the lake in a chair. Her head was slouched to the side.

I ran from the room.

When I reached the lake, I was winded. I bent over, with my hands on my knees, and heaved big breaths, before I could call out.

She was drifting in the middle of the five-acre lake. An insulated cup was in a holder beside her arm. She must have heard me, though, because she raised her head and squinted at me. "What?"

"Sorry. I thought you may have gotten too much sun and fainted from dehydration."

She pushed herself up in the chair. "It's okay. I might have if you hadn't wakened me."

"I know who took the skull off the mountain. It's on a shelf at the neighbor's house. I tried to call Blake, but he must be on a call because he didn't answer. I wanted to take the thing while I was there, but I thought it would be better to let Blake get it. He's busy, but if he could, I think he would want to get it. I want you to go with me to distract the daughter and Ms. Overstreet while I take it."

The lounge chair wobbled, creating ripples in the water, and Janene sat straight up. "Have you lost your mind? You're asking me to participate in a burglary! Besides, it may not be the same one. It could be a fake Plaster of Paris replica."

I sighed and said, "It's the same one I found on Rosa Leigh's property. How many human skulls can be floating around on Copperhead Road? It belongs to her."

Janene cupped her hands around her mouth and yelled as if I was having trouble hearing her. "You wouldn't carry it off the mountain, so how are you planning to bring it home?"

"I'll take gloves."

"No, I won't be your look-out. You call your Sheriff boyfriend and ask him to go with you," she said, dismissing me by reclining back against the chair and closing her eyes.

Disappointed, I returned to the house for my phone.

The sun had gone behind the mountain, and I knew it wouldn't be long until dark. Back inside the house, I tried Blake's office phone, hoping he might be there.

"Did you cook me dinner, or are you inviting me out?" He asked as he finally answered.

"Neither." I blabbed on until my story was told. "I want you to pick me up, and we will rescue Rosa Leigh's skull."

He chuckled. "It's not Rosa Leigh's. She's still living."

"Stop it, Blake Sheets. Drive your behind out here, pronto."

He coughed. *Oops.* That meant he was upset. Or worse, he was angry.

"I will, but you are not going. This is official police business."

My head felt like it would explode any moment, and I yelled, "You arrest her for stealing then!"

Papers shuffled on the other end, and a pen or pencil hit his desk. Finally, he said, "Ives, if she says there is no skull and refuses to let me search for it, I need probable cause to enter her house. So far, you are the only one who has seen this skull. It's your word against hers."

My stomach churned, but I kept my voice calm. "I showed you the photo of the skull. We have proof it was originally on Rosa Leigh's property. How many human skulls have you seen just laying around?"

He sighed. "The picture could have been taken anywhere. There are caves all over the mountains, and I didn't see the skull when I rescued you."

"Rosa Leigh's grandson saw both, and he took the snapshot." The veins in my neck throbbed. "Ms. Overstreet's daughter is in on this."

After a long pause on the other end, he asked, "In on what? You didn't see her take the skull, and she wasn't there when the men took you. When I catch them, I can arrest them for attempted murder and kidnapping, but not her."

"You're not going to go and question her?"

"Yes, I'll be at her house in fifteen or twenty minutes. I'll ask her if she found the skull. And if she says she did, I'll ask to have it for testing. If she says there is no skull, I have no grounds to search her house."

Thoughts flitted through my head. "I'll meet you there. I'll take Simon for another walk before dark."

"Ives, don't you dare go near that house," he said, his voice full of panic.

"I'll take the path through the woods and wait for you behind the house," I said and disconnect our call before he could say anything else about it.

My cell rang again.

I let it go to voicemail.

Chapter 17

I tiptoed to Rosa Leigh's bedroom and eased open the door. Simon was still on the floor beside the bed, and his head snapped up. My friend still had her comforter pulled over her ears. I whispered her name, but she didn't hear me.

"Let's go for your evening walk, Simon."

He rose, and his claws clicked across the wood floor. When he reached the door, he looked up at me with those sad eyes. I bent down and burrowed my face in his soft fur. His head lowered, and I stood. He click-clacked through the hall and waited for me at the door.

Outside, I rushed around the house, crossed the lawn and headed down the road. Simon kept pace beside me. I was hoping I could make it to the woods before Blake caught me.

The sun was lower in the sky, and the late evening air was cooler. I couldn't hear any birds chirping or cawing. Maybe they were perched for the night. I veered left at the edge of the trees, circled the end of the pond and ran towards the woods.

A roar and the sound of crunching stones echoed through the air as Blake whizzed by us.

I can make it to the tree line before he circles the bend and turns into the drive.

I ran, and my companion trotted right next to me.

As Blake slammed his truck door, Simon and I reached the opening. When the Sheriff walked out of sight, I sprinted across the back yard, opened the screen door and tiptoed across the floor to the shelf.

My heart stopped.

It was gone!

In its place was a ceramic pitcher.

In a panic, I slid things around on the dusty middle shelf, tiptoed to check the top one and then heard, "Are you looking for something, dear?"

I pivoted and stared, mouth open. Stammering, I said, "I think I left my water bottle."

Ms. Overstreet shook her head. "I distinctly remember. You put it in your back pack before you took my arm to help me earlier."

I cocked my head to one side.

What gives with this woman? She appears alert now, and her memory seems accurate, the opposite of this afternoon.

She cleared her throat. "Would you like my daughter to help you look?" A mischievous grin spread across her face. "I'd help, but I can't see so well anymore."

Turning, I said, "I thought I set it on the shelf."

I scanned the area again as I walked toward the door. "Don't disturb her. I probably left it somewhere on one of my hikes. It's one of Rosa Leigh's insulated containers, and I want to find it." I opened the screen door.

"I know how to keep secrets, too," Ms. Overstreet said. She fidgeted with a button on her blouse. "Better run, dear, my daughter and the Sheriff are walking through the house."

I bounced down the two steps and whispered for Simon to follow. We rushed across the plush grass to the woods.

A quiet dusk was settling over Copperhead Ridge. Inside the trees, it was dark, like someone had turned off the lights. My footsteps mingled with a rush of wind through the trees. The floor felts spongy, and the fragrance of pine filled the air. Occasionally, a pinecone cracked beneath my feet. The wooded area wasn't long, and thankfully, we reached the pond area soon.

The stars and full moon lit the way around the water. Bull frogs croaking echoed back and forth, and the familiar fishy smell filled the air. Soon, the lighter color of the pavement came into view and stones crunched beneath my feet. I slowed to a fast walk to catch my breath, and we made it to the house and inside without seeing Blake.

I crept back to the bedroom to check on Rosa Leigh. She stirred.

"Do you want me to fix you something to eat?" I asked.

She raised her head and looked at me through sleepy eyes. "Maybe some oatmeal. There's an assorted box in the cupboard. See if there's any cinnamon and nut left. If not, any of the others will do. I'll be out as soon as I use the bathroom and splash some water on my face."

I walked to the end of the hallway and rapped on the door to the mother-in-law quarters.

"Come in," Janene said.

I opened the door.

She is in the recliner next to the French doors.

"Rosa Leigh and I are having oatmeal. Would you like me to fix you a dish and a couple pieces of toast?"

She lifted her brown hair off her shoulders, let it fall again and asked, "We're not going out for dinner?"

I shook my head.

"Rosa Leigh's been in bed since she returned. Is she okay?"

I hadn't told Janene the sad news. "Our friend isn't feeling well."

I closed the door fast, so Janene couldn't ask any more questions and made my way back to the kitchen. Simon trailed behind me like a puppy wanting to be near his mommy.

"I'll put your food down first, boy." He looked up at me and waited.

I was placing his dish of food and water in his spot by the back door when Rosa Leigh and Janene strolled in. I washed my hands and cooked Rosa Leigh's oatmeal first. Then Janene's and mine. We were about to say grace when the doorbell rang. I knew who was there.

"Janene, would you see who is at the door?" I asked, trying to act as if I didn't have a care in the world.

Her eyes grew big and her mouth opened. "Its dark out there. I think we need the gun."

Rosa Leigh slid off her bar stool. "I'll go." She went to a closet and took out a wood baseball bat. "Who is it?"

A muffled voice seeped under the door. "It's Blake."

Rosa Leigh opened the door. "What brings you here this late, Sheriff?"

He stepped inside and took off his hat. The skin below his hairline was creased from the weight of the rim. "I came to deliver some news to Ives."

Rosa Leigh motioned him inside and closed the door. "She's in the kitchen. Would you like a bowl of oatmeal?"

He placed his hat on a chair, followed her into the kitchen, and sat at the bar. "I'll take a hot cup of coffee. I know you always stock it," he said and grinned at Rosa Leigh. "We spend our lives remaking ourselves, but some habits never change, do they?"

Rosa Leigh returned to her oatmeal. "No, they don't."

I put a coffee pod in the pot, pushed the button and waited until the stream of brown liquid stopped. "Fixing a cup of coffee is certainly easier than when we were in school." I carried the steaming brew to Blake and placed it on the counter in front of him.

He looked up at me with his brilliant blue eyes, and my stomach twittered. "Ms. Overstreet's daughter took me to the back porch, Ives. There was no skull on those shelves. They claim neither of them saw one. I've done what you asked, and now you are going to do what I want."

"I will," I said, but not without crossing my fingers behind my back.

Unless I find a new lead.

"Can we search the mountain tomorrow?" I asked.

Blake's shoulders sagged. "If I'm not bogged down with work."

I know the way.

Chapter 18

Early the next morning, as I opened the back door, Rosa Leigh entered the kitchen rubbing her eyes. "Where do you think you're going?"

I glanced at her over my shoulder. "Simon and I are going hiking. We should be back by noon, or a little after."

She rushed to the door and slammed it. "No, you are not. Today is Art on Wheels Day."

I crossed my arms across my chest and puffed a white strand of hair off my forehead. "So?"

"I need you and Janene to help today. Jersey Donovan called and says she's sick, and Nettie received a reservation for fifty people for the County Commissioners' meeting."

I raised one eyebrow. "You know I am not artistic."

She smacked my arm. "You are, too. You bake the best desserts in the country." Rosa Leigh put a cup beneath the brewer, the K-cup in the hole, and pushed the button. "And you can cook when you want to."

I tapped one foot. "I follow directions and dump flour, sugar, vanilla, eggs and milk in a bowl and slather canned frosting on the layers." I leaned close to her until I could almost touch her nose. "It is not art."

She did her famous palm wave. "You attended art classes in high school and college. It won't matter. The seniors desire visitors more than the activity anyway." She pointed to the hallway. "Please wake Janene. I hope she hasn't started writing yet. I really need her help."

I wanted to tell Rosa Leigh to shove her Art on Wheels, but I knew she needed the distraction. If we didn't help, she might have to cancel. I trudged to Janene's room like a good girl and rapped on her door.

"Come in."

I stepped inside, eased the door closed and told her of Rosa Leigh's lamebrain idea.

Janene smiled. "Sounds like fun. I haven't done any art since college.

My heart sank to my toes. I was hoping she'd say no, and then I wouldn't feel guilty if Rosa Leigh canceled. "For you, it will be fun. For me, it will be torture. I can't stay inside the lines in a coloring book. My own children tried over and over to teach me how to draw and paint. I couldn't. Don't you want to stay here and write?"

Janene grinned and rushed to the shower.

I sighed, and I went to my room.

Maybe I'll run into Blake. With that thought, I changed out of hiking boots, jeans and long-sleeved shirt into a pair of denim blue capris and a lose-fitting blue and white striped gauze blouse. I smeared foundation on my face, darkened my invisible eyebrows to gray and lined my eyes with smoke blue. I put on pale pink lipstick to give them some life, brushed my hair, sprayed it and went into the kitchen to wait.

When the other two arrived, Rosa Leigh motioned for us to follow.

She went out the back door and into the pool house, opened a two-door metal cupboard containing shelves of plastic containers, all sizes and shapes, and handed two rectangular boxes to Janene, who carried them to the car. Rosa Leigh handed me two plastic boxes about three feet long and two feet high each.

"What's in these things? They're heavy."

She talked as she closed the doors. "You are carrying the containers of paint. Janene took the canvases and paper."

I looked at Rosa Leigh's empty arms. "And where is your load?"

There's a mischievous twinkle in her eyes. "You and Janene are carrying all the supplies."

She sashayed to the car, and like an obedient servant, I trailed her. *What one does for a friend.*

The clock on the car dash read 9:00. As I closed the door, the wind blew hot and humid air inside. "The leaves are turned over, and Mom always said it would rain when they turn that way."

Rosa Leigh watched in her rearview mirror and backed out. "We need rain. Maybe it'll cool the air." She straightened her wheels and accelerated, causing my head to smack against the head rest.

As we snaked around the winding road, the sun filtered through the leaves, making strange shadows on the pavement. Trees gave way to rock cliffs. Those disappeared, and we were in flat land with the mountain silhouetted in the background.

Rosa Leigh's speed had the pine and white hickory trees whizzing by the window. We passed pastures with men and boys on tractors in the fields and children romping in the yards. The scenes brought back many memories, some good, others less welcome. And then, we passed through Three Pines.

The village with its two streets, one grocery store, Nettie's restaurant, a funeral home and a handful of churches hadn't grown in the forty years I'd been gone. The jobs went south years ago to cheaper labor, according to factory owners. My dad worked in the brick yard twenty-five years, and my mother worked in the sewing factory for fifteen. They made minimum wage, worked long hours with no overtime, no insurance or vacation time. Those who could leave, did. The others commuted or scratched out a living the best they could.

Lost in thought, the time and distance zipped by, and we were winding up a narrow street, blanketed by trees on both sides, to the Senior Enrichment Retirement Center. The building was once a golf retreat for those who could afford to play the game.

Rosa Leigh parked the car, and we filed out. She opened the trunk and filled our arms with boxes of supplies. Janene and I followed her through the double door and down a long hallway, smelling of a pine cleaning agent, into a large room with round tables and chairs filled with older men and women.

Rosa Leigh chirped, "Good Morning, Friends!"

She was bubbly, like before the diagnosis.

The crowd echoed back a greeting.

"Ives, you put your supplies on those two tables over there," Rosa Leigh said and swept her hand in the direction she wanted me to go with them. "Janene, you take yours to the other two."

I hurried to the closest table and squeezed in between a woman and a man. As I leaned to reach the center of the table, a hand squeezed my behind. I sat the supplies on the table, turned and whacked the hand.

A silver-haired man rubbed the back of his palm. He smiled and tilted his head. "It was worth it," he said and chuckled.

I locked eyes with him. "Do you grab all the women's -"

He yelled for Rosa Leigh. "Your helper is using foul language."

She stared daggers at me, and I shook my head in disbelief. When she turned her back, I grabbed the other box. As I passed the butt grabber, I pinched his cheek.

He yelped.

"Touch me again, and I'll squeeze your body part that will have you singing soprano the rest of your life!"

I made my way to the other table. Seated around were gentlemen, women and I hoped no butt squeezers.

As I placed a box of supplies in the center of the table, the room erupted into cheers and clapping. I followed the lady's eyes next to me. Red and Elizabeth walked in, smiling and waving. I continued removing art supplies from the boxes and put them on the table. A lady across from me, with plum-colored hair, asked, "What's your name?"

I opened my mouth and Rosa Leigh darted past saying, "Read the name tag, Gilda."

She squinted her green eyes and said, "There's no Schnepe around here. Where are you from?"

I straightened the pile of lose watercolor sheets on the table. "I live in Florida. I grew up here, though, and my best friend then and now is Rosa Leigh."

The gray-haired man next to Gilda asked, "Are you staying with Ms. Rosa Leigh?"

I nodded, and like my college art instructor once did, I sorted all the paint brushes in piles by size. I handed each person a watercolor box, filled with the primary colors, took out the plastic butter and yogurt bowls and handed two to each person seated around the table. "I know the lady with the gorgeous plum hair is Gilda. What's your name?" I asked the man seated to her right.

He glanced up at me. "Malcomb," he replied. "Are you staying long?"

I scratched the back of my neck, thinking about how much I wanted to reveal. "I'm not certain. There's a hurricane in Florida right now, and the place where I live was evacuated."

The gentleman seated on the right of Malcomb spoke up. "I'm Paul, and let's quit all the talking and paint. I like to paint."

I observed his facial features. He had sunken cheeks, and his gray hair was streaked with brown. Most of the other people in the room had snow-white hair.

Another gentleman seated next to the complainer said, "Hold your horses, Paul. This lady is new, so don't be rude if you want her to help you." He looked at me, smiled, and his green eyes twinkled. "I'm Herbert. I'm a widower, and I'm looking for my next wife."

I smiled. "Keep looking. I'm a widow, too, but I'm not interested in remarrying." He grabbed his bowls and brushes and pulled them closer.

I made eye contact with the others seated around the table. "I placed all you need within arm's reach. What's your name?" I asked the woman seated next to Herbert.

Her head went down. "Evelyn." Her voice was soft, almost inaudible.

The woman to her right chimed in. "I'm Delores, and I hate art day."

Paul leaned forward in his chair. "Because you stink at it. You're not careful to stay in the lines and slap paint everywhere and anywhere."

I walked around to the woman and patted her on the back. "It's okay. I'm not good at art, either."

Paul jumped up, turning over his chair. "Ms. Rosa Leigh, I want to change tables. This teacher can't paint."

I shushed him. "I didn't say I can't paint. I said I'm not great at it."

Someone clapped their hands, and I jerked my head in the direction of the sound.

Rosa Leigh stood across the room at another table with one hand raised.

The voices stopped.

"Let's begin, folks. There is a piece of red tracing paper on your table and a photo of a beach scene, a sailboat in the distance and a palm tree in the foreground. Who remembers what you do first?"

Hands popped up all over the room. Rosa Leigh called out a name, and the woman yelled, "We tape the picture to the paper, put the tracing paper under it and take one of the red pens and trace it."

Rosa Leigh clapped. "Great job, Tilly!"

Delores reached for a photo and mumbled, "Suck up."

I smiled. Every crowd had a suck up and a Delores personality. I noticed Evelyn struggling to reach the paper and handed her a sheet. She said, "Why don't you be a dearie and pass the supplies out like the other helpers do?"

I grimaced. "It will be good exercise for you. Reaching is a good way to stay flexible."

Evelyn narrowed her eyes at me. "Stop blabbering and hand me my tools."

Malcomb mumbled, "Why do you think she looks like a whale?"

Gilda giggled, kicked his leg, and he kicked her back.

Pent-up anger was rising, so I took a deep breath and blew it out. "Do I need to treat you like children and put you in time-out?"

Malcom laughed. "Can't do it. Delores will sit out the whole time because she doesn't like art. Ms. Rosa Leigh sends most of us to our room if we become incorrigible, but not Delores. She has to complete the assignment."

"And if Ms. D decides not to complete the work, what then?" I asked.

They shook their heads and kept working. I decided not to probe any further.

Evelyn finished tracing and put her pen in the center. "I need a check."

I looked at her and shrugged, wondering what she meant.

She rolled her eyes and said, "You need to see if I have traced around everything I need to in the photo."

"Okay." I walked to her and looked at her tracing from top to bottom and side to side.

Evelyn tugged at my sleeve. "There's a lot of crazy stuff happening on Copperhead Ridge. You be careful, and you tell Ms. Rosa Leigh to buy herself a gun."

"Tell me more," I whispered, suddenly much happier to be part of art day.

Paul scooted his chair back. The screech pierced my ears and pain radiated to my brain. He snatched a pail from the center of the table and said, "I'm finished. I'll bring the water today."

When he entered the men's room, I asked Evelyn, "How long have you been a resident here?"

She pulled two plastic containers to her. "Five years, and Paul has visitors every Sunday. Long time ago, he controlled the shine and drug business around here. His nickname is Shine. His oldest son took over when he got put in here and brings his daddy an update every week. I put together puzzles in the community room, and it's around the corner from Paul's."

She grabbed a spray bottle, squirted each tub of color and continued, "I couldn't hear what's going on, but they're scared. A man came to Three Pines who is in the Cartel. He claimed Copperhead Ridge and warned Paul's family. 'Course they didn't listen, and one of the brothers got hurt bad as a warning."

She looked up as if to make sure no one was listening to their conversation. "Come to my room on Sunday, and I'll tell you more." She cocked her head to where she could more than likely see my worried face. "You might hear them talking yourself." Her finger went to her lips, and she clammed up.

I circled the table, helping the others. Paul returned and dipped each container in the bucket of water and passed two to each person. He had a seat and painted.

"Do you need help?" I asked.

"Not from you," he said. "You painted Delores' sky red in spots."

My shoulders stiffened. "I showed her how to take the color out until it was pink. It looks like a pink sunset."

He brushed from side-to-side on his sky. "Everyone knows a sky is blue."

"Sunsets have red skies sometime," I said. "And artists have something called an artistic license to create a scene the way they want."

"This is not a sunset scene. It's broad daylight."

I sighed. "You look familiar. What's your last name?"

"Overstreet," he said. "But we've never met. I remember faces and names."

When I caught my breath, I asked, "Are you related to Ms. Overstreet on Copperhead Ridge?"

He nodded. "My sister."

Ah ha! I'm more convinced than ever that Ms. Overstreet and her daughter are involved in the missing skull, but what does it have to do with drugs and moonshine? Maybe she's not as feebleminded as she wants me to believe, and she has lucid moments. I won't have time today, but I'll stop by her house tomorrow and take her for a walk to the pond to tire her. When I take her back to the house, I'll fix her a cup of the herbal tea she claims helps her sleep. I'll then have the run of her house.

What can go wrong if she is sleeping?

Chapter 19

The next morning, I rose early and did my usual routine preparation for the day's hike, with two changes. I slipped a flashlight and four bottles of water into my bag, and put Rosa Leigh's pocket-knife in my jeans—the one she kept in the drawer of the stand by the front door. I also shoved two Sleepy Time tea bags into my backpack along with a pound of colored M&Ms.

The microwave clock said it was 7:00 A.M. when Simon and I made it outside.

I decided to go up the mountain first since I wasn't certain what time Ms. Overstreet's daughter left for work. I didn't want to waste time staking out the place.

The morning air was heavy with the scent of the alfalfa Rosa Leigh's neighbor had cut the day before, and the brisk wind was blowing the odor up the hollow. As I walked past the lake and back to the woods, dewdrops glistened on the grass. I was glad I'd put my jeans inside my hiking boots as it had rained a lot lately, and the weeds were waist high at the edge of the woods.

Simon jumped over the taller ones and sprinted up the incline. The sun peeked through the clouds and filtered through the branches. The air had just a hint of fall coolness, but it would still heat up fast since there were few clouds.

A melody of chirps and tweets echoed through the hush of the wind in the treetops. The path I'd made before was no longer as distinct due to the extra growth from the rain. The ground was spongy with moisture, and I checked each step before I put my full weight into it. Like before, the gnarled undergrowth grabbed at my legs, causing me to stumble.

Here beneath the trees, some of the grass was dry and prickly. I stopped often and listened for sounds. Other than nature and my own huffs and puffs, it was quiet. When a woodpecker tapped into a tree, I nearly jumped out of my skin. Simon ignored it, though, and romped ahead.

When I was close to the cave, I stopped again to listen for human sounds. I didn't hear any which was good.

The clouds had given way to sunlight, and the air was smothering hot. If my grumbling stomach was an indication, I'd guess it was close to noon, or a little later. I decided to go ahead and eat now that we'd arrived.

I can hide behind the same trees where Simon and I hid before and have lunch.

I set the backpack in the tall grass surrounding the oak and unloaded our food. Simon seemed to sense the danger we were in being on the mountain. He hadn't barked once, not even when he chased a rabbit.

As we ate, two huge buzzards peered at us from a branch high in the tree. Their beady eyes sent a shiver through me. I hoped they were wanting our food and not us for their lunch. They didn't make a peep. Katy-dids chirped, birds cawed, others trilled, but the buzzards just stared at us. Simon watched them, too, waiting for one to dart close to the ground.

I finished my sandwich, gulped a half bottle of water and packed the trash. I didn't want to leave any signs to indicate I'd been there. I ventured from our safe place into the open area.

The dry creek bed of charcoal gray slate didn't reveal any footprints. I searched the path to the right. The grass and shrubs were recently broken, but the other side was unchanged from our last trip.

I took out my cell and checked the time. It was 12:45 P.M. and all was well. The men may have been there the day before. And I hoped they were and that they'd left something for me to know they had been. With a little luck, I could be in and out, though, before they returned. I crossed my fingers and scrambled to the top of the hill where I'd seen the skull.

The vegetation looked undisturbed. I searched around all the bushes, shrubs and dead leaves. Nothing! The tall pole was still standing. The mason jar was in the same place, buried halfway into the soil.

I walked over the hill to the mouth of the cave, listened for human noises, observed the area and whispered to the dog, "Come on, we're going treasure hunting."

He looked up at me, but his usual grin left his face. He whimpered.

Do dogs have premonitions?

Before our trip this particular day, I had researched caves and their habitat. My parents hadn't raised a fool.

I crept into the dank, musty smelling cavern. The sunlight was shining into the opening, but as I trekked further back into the twilight zone, the light grew dimmer.

Trogloxenes lived in this area, near the entrance, and these animals needed to go outside for food. But the fellows gave me the creeps. They included rats, raccoons, bats and bears. Since it was early Fall, I wasn't afraid of coming upon a bear. The rats and bats, however, terrified me.

I opened the bag of candy and turned on my trusty flashlight. Simon brushed past, nearly knocking me off balance. "Oh, you want to lead now, do you?"

He looked back and waited for me.

As we entered the transition ecozone, I began to drop the M&Ms. Chocolate was one food Simon wouldn't touch, and I was hoping none of the other varmints would, either. The natural light was almost nonexistent, but if I turned off my flashlight, there was still a smidgeon. The dog led us deeper into complete darkness.

The humidity was extremely high, at least ninety-five percent. According to my research, this would be where the true cave animals lived. I wasn't afraid of them, except in complete darkness when they scurried all over the rocks. They had no pigment or sight, and they were slow moving due to their metabolic rate. They had highly-specialized auditory organs, sensitive hearing and jumped at the slightest sound...thus all the maddening scurrying.

When we reached a fork in the channels, Simon waited for my direction. I nudged him to the right. He and I wandered through the passageway awhile, but there were no signs of humans. I turned and went back to the other fork.

We wandered into a large room with low-hanging stalagmites and tall stalactites. Puddles of water filled the low spots, and to the right, a stream gurgled over rocks. Recognizing the sound from the day I almost didn't make it out alive, my heart skipped a beat. I dropped candy and pushed on until the pathway narrowed, and the opening was only knee-level.

I hadn't crawled through any parts of the cave with the men on nearly disastrous trip and realized this was new territory. I skimmed the walls with the light. Another arm opened on the other side. I walked to that channel and shined the light inside.

Simon growled.

I patted his head, not certain whether he felt danger or heard one of the creatures stirring.

I glanced at my cell and noticed we'd been inside the cave for an hour. "Okay, boy, we'll search these other pathways another time."

He darted back the way we came. I followed.

The return went much faster. Simon followed his scent, ignoring my markers, and so I picked up the tiny pieces. The sunlight glaring through the opening hurt my eyes, and I shielded them over the brows with my hand. Simon stopped at the cave mouth, turned and waited for me.

"Is there anyone out there?" I asked him.

He waited.

I tiptoed to where he stood and listened. When I heard no sounds of the men, I stuck my head out and then sprinted for the trees, my backpack bouncing hard against my body. Out of breath, I collapsed on the ground. Simon was next to me, panting. The quick change in the air temperature and the jog had winded both of us.

I finally quit heaving air and emptied a bottle of water into a container for Simon. He lapped up the stream flowing in. I drank half of the last bottle before it dawned on me, we might need it before we got home. I placed the bottle and the container in the pack, and we started our descent.

An hour later, I stepped from the leaf canopy into the hot August afternoon sun. Sweat was dripping from my hair, and poor Simon's tongue was lolling out. "Come on, boy. We'll take Ms. Overstreet for a walk, and while she's resting from the walk to the pond, I'll let you go for a swim."

Rosa Leigh, Janene and Blake's stern warnings were inside my head, reminding me of the dangers on this mountain. Or perhaps it was my angel. But I ignored all of them.

After Ms. Overstreet's walk and a cup of herbal tea, she'll sleep like a baby. Besides, I'm performing a good deed helping her exercise in the fresh air and sunlight.

Even if she wakes, how can an old woman hurt me?

Chapter 20

Simon and I arrived at Ms. Overstreet's, and I pushed the doorbell. Soft chimes resonated through the house.

"One moment," she said.

When she opened the door, I gasped, as I hadn't heard her making her way towards us.

"You're running early today, Merlene," she said.

I stepped closer, having no idea who Merlene was. "It's Ives, Ms. Overstreet. Simon and I were out for an afternoon walk and wondered if you would like to go back to the pond with us."

"Who are you?" She asked, squinting at me.

"Ives, Rosa Leigh Adams' friend. I brought you home from the cemetery last week. Remember?"

She studied my face and looked down at Simon. "Aw, yes, I remember the dog loved the water." She stepped back a few steps and opened the door wider. "Come on in. I must have nodded off, and it takes me awhile to clear the fog when I wake. I need to fetch some shoes. I can't walk outside in these house slippers." She shuffled back through the living room to the hallway. "Be a dear and close the door."

I looked around, but, of course, no one in their right mind would hide a skull in plain sight of visitors who they knew were interested in finding it.

She returned wearing athletic shoes and walked through the kitchen and out onto the screened porch. Simon and I followed. She seemed to have forgotten we were there. She walked down the two steps and hobbled across the yard. As I hurried to catch her, Simon ran ahead of us. About halfway through the woods, she stopped, turned and said, "I forgot my walking stick. I can't make it there and back today without my walking stick."

"Take my arm." I held it out for her, and she grabbed it. "You didn't have your walking stick the last time."

She glanced at me out of the corner of her eye. "It wasn't scorching hot out that day." With her other hand, she reached into her pocket, snatched a tissue and rubbed it against her nose. "Pollen's bad today."

"I hadn't noticed."

"When you're my age, you will. The harvesting keeps the pollen stirred up this time a year." She scratched the back of her neck. "We must be back before Danita gets home. She doesn't like me to leave the house when she's not here. Says she'll put me in a nursing home if I keep doing it." She stopped, sighed a long breath and continued, "Growing old's not for sissies."

Simon was waist deep in the pond, grinning at us when we arrived. Ms. Overstreet staggered to the bench and basically fell into it. "Lands sakes alive, its hotter than blue blazes out here. Can't stay long. I forgot my bonnet."

I sat beside her and said, "We'll be home before your daughter arrives."

She sniffed. "Smart as a tack, that one, . . . knows if I've left the house." She fanned her face and looked at me. "Its mighty nice of you to bring an old lady to her favorite place. Thank you."

"You're welcome. I wouldn't want to stay inside all day without sunshine, and Simon and I walk every day. While I'm visiting, I can bring you here anytime you want."

She dabbed her forehead and beneath her nose with a tissue. "I think I need to go back. It's too hot." She scooted forward, rocked three times and stood. "I can make it back if you want to let the dog enjoy the water longer."

But I was more than delighted to take her to the house. I'd have more time to search without worrying about Danita coming home and catching me. "I'll bring him back and let him play after you're settled at home." I took her arm and called Simon. He waded out of the water and shook, spraying the grass around him.

The three of us ambled back through the woods. Simon chased moles, birds and everything else he saw, but Ms. Overstreet appeared not to notice anything, except the ground. Her head was bowed, and her eyes were focused on where her feet would land. I supposed that was how things were when you were older.

We finally made it back and into the house, and Ms. Overstreet sank onto her sofa. In between uneasy breaths, she said, "Will you bring me a cold glass of water from the fridge, dear?"

"Sure, and I like a calming cup of tea in the afternoon. I'll make us a cup."

Fixing tea will give me a legitimate reason to search the cupboards.

In the kitchen, I took off my backpack, found the tea I'd packed and made two cups. While the microwave was running, I looked in every nook and cranny, but I couldn't find the skull. When the tea was ready, I hurried into the living room.

"Here you go, Ms. Overstreet. Sip your tea and tell me more about your family. How many children do you have?"

She blew the hot liquid. "Six living. One died when she was a baby. Hand me the photo album on the bottom of the coffee table. I'll show you my family." Within fifteen minutes, her words were slurring and her head nodding. "Where are my manners. I can't stay awake."

Taking her cup and placing it in the saucer on the coffee table, I said, "Let me help you stretch out." I lifted her legs onto the sofa. As I placed a pillow beneath her head, she moaned.

As soon as she was snoring, I crept to the hallway and into the first room on the right. It looked like it might be hers. A small wooden jewelry box sat on top of a chest. Inside were gaudy necklaces and rings. Her ratty house coat hung across the back of a chair, and the air smelled like rose water. There was no skull lurking on any of the furniture. So, I opened the walk-in closet and stepped inside. No skull.

I wandered to the next room. I'm in the closet reaching up for a shoebox when someone said, "Why are you rummaging through the closet?"

Startled, I pivoted.

Ms. Overstreet's daughter was standing in the open doorway, holding a gun. Simon was also inside the room, his tail between his legs.

My hands went up. "I . . . I was looking for a blanket to put over your mother."

She eased backward and waved the gun, an invitation for me to exit the room. "There is one folded on her bed. You couldn't miss it. Why did you search through our rooms?"

My brain froze. I couldn't think of a logical reason.

She flicked her gun toward the living room. "Out of the closet and out of here." She waved the gun again toward the living room.

I went.

"The Sheriff will be here soon. I called him."

"If you'll let me, I can explain."

Her head jerked toward the road and to the sound of tires grinding stone. "Don't bother. You can tell the story to him." She side-stepped to the door, her eyes darting to the drive and then back at me.

Seconds passed. She pushed open the storm door.

Blake stepped inside, and his eyes grew large.

"There she is, Sheriff. I had a camera installed several months ago to watch Momma. I'll give you the video to use in court. The strange woman took her from the house and was gone a long time. When she brought her back, she waited for Momma to fall asleep and searched through our house."

I didn't try to explain. I put my hands behind my back, walked to Blake and stopped for him to put on handcuffs.

He opened the storm door wide and pushed me out. "Stop being silly and wait in the car."

Walking out the door, Simon behind me, I kicked at the stones all the way to the car.

Chapter 21

Blake's jaw was clenched, and his eyes were flashing anger when he returned to the squad car. He started the engine and spun gravel as he backed out. To make certain I didn't attempt to talk to him, he cranked up the radio.

There were no glances in the rearview mirror, or a word uttered, the whole way back to the station. When I tried to engage him in a conversation, he turned the radio volume even higher. I put my hands over my ears to block the sound, but the noise level remained awful all the way to Three Pines.

At the office, his brakes squealed when we stopped, and I was propelled forward against the seat belt. He parked, flipped his hat on his head and walked to the back of the car to open the door for me.

I slid out and tried to smile at him, but his cold blue eyes were staring over my head at the building. In an extravagant wave, he swept his hand toward the door.

I sloughed around the car, walked to the door and opened it myself.

"Did you leave Gentleman Blake at home today?" I asked and smiled.

"No, I did not," he said, and hitched his head to the room with bars...the cell.

I stared at him in stunned disbelief. "You're kidding."

He folded his arms across his chest and shook his head.

"I didn't break any laws! Ms. Overstreet let me into the house."

He jerked his thumb towards the cell.

"You're being unreasonable," I said and stepped closer to him. "Putting me in jail is ridiculous! What crime will you charge me with?"

He jerked his head hard toward the cell.

But I was not about to make it easy for him. I sat in his desk chair.

In a flash, he crossed the distance between us and wheeled me into the cell.

The slam of the door and the deadening click of the lock chilled me.

When he then stormed out of the building, panic rose from deep inside my stomach. My breaths were coming in ragged gulps. I let my hands fall into my lap, bowed my head and attempted to pray, but my thoughts bounced all over the place. I paced the small cinder-block room.

God is angry with me, too, because time seems to be standing still. How does anyone spend time in this place and then go back out on the street and continue to do the same crimes? There is no privacy in here. How do the women use the toilet if men are present?

I looked at the urinal, the commode, the wash basin and the flimsy cot. There only two views – the interior office and the street outside – and, the latter, was only visible if you were standing on the bed and looking through the dirty small window.

I paced some more. I sat awhile on the sheet-less mattress. It was hard as a rock, and the springs hurt my butt. I thought of all the drunks, druggies and heaven only knows who else had slept on that bed, and I sprung up. Thank goodness I wouldn't have to spend the night. I paced again, until my legs grew tired and then took refuge in Blake's chair.

Finally, after what seemed like forever, a door slammed, heavy feet thudded across the floor, and Blake's hat rung the hook on the wall above his desk. He walked into my view, crossed to his desk and stared my way. I think he wanted to sit, but I was in his chair.

I smiled. "I'll share."

His eyes narrowed and his scowl deepened. "This is not funny. Ms. Overstreet's daughter is coming in later to press charges against you for breaking and entering."

I jumped out of his chair and grabbed the bars. "It won't do her any good! I told you I didn't break in. And there's no law against me entering if I'm invited," I said, my voice rising with each word. "And I was!"

He marched to the bars and glared at me. "Were you invited to rummage through everything in the house? What did you expect to find?"

I moved to where I could look him in the eye. "You couldn't search for the skull legally. I was doing you a favor."

Blake grabbed his head with both hands and turned, leaving his back toward me. "They may not have it. If they do, you made them suspicious the night you were snooping on the porch. Ms. Overstreet might be old and senile, but she can still talk and repeat what she saw." He spun back around. "I can't charge you with breaking and entering, you're right, but you also had no right to look through their house. If I can't talk her out of this——"

"I didn't do anything wrong!" I grasped two bars and stuck my nose between them. "I didn't steal anything, nor did I take or borrow anything. I went empty-handed, and I left the same way. What can you charge me with?"

He blew out a long breath and paced. "How about being a public menace?"

My heart thumped. Concern was written all over his face. "Nuisance," I said, trying to lighten the mood. "And you didn't search me, so you don't know if I took anything or not."

He walked to the hook on the wall, grabbed the keys and returned. Unlocking the door, he motioned for me to walk into the office area.

I waggled my finger for him to come in where I stood.

He lunged at me and pulled me into the office area. "I can't believe you! Is everything a game to you? Pull your pockets out."

As he searched me, a whiff of his spicy, masculine cologne warmed me all over. I looked at his crinkled forehead and realized how much stress I was causing him. "I'm sorry," I whispered.

He rubbed his face. "I know, but not nearly as sorry as you will be if I can't find a way to talk Danita out of pressing charges."

"When will she be here?"

"Anytime." He nodded, basically telling me to go back into the cell.

I did.

He grabbed his chair, backed out of the cell, locked the door and wheeled the chair to his desk.

I caught a glimpse of something streak by the front window. The door opened, and the woman I'd seen at Ms. Overstreet's house entered, leading her mother.

Two against one. What kind of trouble have I gotten myself into?

Chapter 22

The younger woman closed the door and walked across the room. Primed to explode, her eyes revealed her pent-up anger.

"Sorry to take so long," she said. "The doctor's office was full, and Mother's appointment took longer than expected." She helped her mother sit down in the chair in front of Blake's desk and turned back to him. "Do you have the paperwork ready for me to sign?"

She was late forties to mid-fifties, pretty, and she knew it. Her green sundress highlighted her green eyes. She fluttered her eye lashes at Blake and smiled innocently.

There's history between Blake and her, or she wants there to be. I swallowed the sour taste filling my mouth.

He returned her smile and placed his thumbs in his belt. "I don't have it ready. You need to write up the incident."

"Why? I gave you the video from the camera." She placed her hands on his desk and leaned over, revealing deep cleavage.

Blake kept eye contact. "I wrote my report, but you have to write the incident up in your own handwriting."

She stood rigid, placed her hands on her hips and leveled her eyes at me. "Give me whatever I need, and I'll write what I witnessed."

Blake strolled around the desk. "You know, Danita," he said, touching her forearm, "I watched the video. Your mother let her and the dog into the house, and your mother went out the back door with Ms. Schnepe and the dog earlier. The three of them returned together."

He pointed at me but kept his eyes focused on hers. "She steeped your mom a cup of tea and drank one with her. There's no visible sign she meant to harm anyone."

Danita's mouth opened.

"Yes, she rummaged through your belongings," he continued. "And, I searched her. She didn't take anything from your house." He swiped his index finger down the bridge of his nose. "Did you give her a chance to explain what she was looking for?"

Way to go, old friend. Use your Sheets' charm. It always worked on me.

Restless, the younger woman's eyes darted from him to me. Her lips pulled into a snarl as she sauntered to my cell. "What were you looking for? Momma's glasses?" Her chin jutted out. "Or perhaps a blanket?"

My fingers were trembling, and my legs wilted like a flower. I took hold of the bars for support.

She walked close to me, wrinkled her nose and eased backward. "Some of us have plans outside the jail tonight." Her sensual perfume filling the air reminded me I hadn't showered or changed after my hike and arrest. Danita cocked her ear towards me and cupped her hand behind it.

I wanted to reach through the metal bars and pull off her darn ear. I just glared at her instead. "I was looking for the skull you stole off Rosa Leigh Adams' property."

She threw up her hands and looked at Blake. "I have no idea what she's talking about."

"Yes, you do. I saw it on a shelf in the screened porch." I knew I should shut up, but I didn't. I flailed my hands through the air and then pointed at her. "When the Sheriff visited you, it was already missing from the shelf." I glanced at Ms. Overstreet, hoping she wouldn't rat me out about searching the shelves while Blake was there. She licked her lips but didn't say a word. I guessed she had visions of a nursing home dancing before her eyes.

Danita marched to Blake's desk. "This woman is unbelievable! How would she know a skull was missing from the shelf if she weren't snooping? Give me the paper."

Blake reached to a file on the side of his desk and took out a packet. "Before you waste your time filling this out, there is no evidence against her." His eyes darted my way and back to Danita. "However, you can file a restraining order to keep her off your property. If she violates it, I can do something then."

Danita patted her foot. "Fine. Give me the form." She remained standing while she wrote. When she finished, she tossed the pen on his desk and turned to me. "I dare you to step back on our place." A smug smile formed on her lips. She took her mother's arm, helped her stand and walked beside the older woman as she shuffled to the door. Neither of them looked back on their way out.

I blew out a long breath. "Can you believe her?"

Blake rubbed his chin, trudged across the room and unlocked my cell. I hurried from my prison as fast as my legs would carry me. "Give me my phone, and I'll call Rosa Leigh to come pick me up."

"I'll drive you. She's at an appointment."

I didn't want another silent treatment with blaring music, and I could tell he was still angry at me. "I'll call Janene. She'll be ticked I interrupted her flow, but she'll come."

"She drove Rosa Leigh to the appointment."

My head shot up. He shifted from one foot to the other, and for the first time, I noticed his eyes were sad. "Rosa Leigh's surgeon called and said he had a cancelation. She's in surgery."

The news sucked the air from my lungs. My insides felt like they would cave in, and I sank to the floor. Before my knees slammed against the wood, Blake caught me. The sobs I'd been holding since I cried on the back of Simon burst through the dam. He half carried me to a chair, snatched tissues from a box on his desk and stuffed them into my hands.

"How long have you known this?" I asked, my words coming out between hiccups.

"If you mean how long I've known about Rosa Leigh's cancer and the surgery, the day after she found out. As for the surgery time itself, not long. While you were in jail, I called her to let her know where you were. She was on her way out the door. She left you a note at the house."

"Oh, Blake," I said and cried. "I let her down. She asked me not to look for the skull for fear the men would hurt me. I didn't listen."

"Do you ever listen to anyone? She knows you. She's forgiven you, and she needs you. I'll run you to the hospital, and for the record, I let you spend the time behind bars to wake you up. This county has one judge, and he's tough on breaking and entering. If Danita pushes this, the B&E won't stick, but she does work for the judge. Who knows what law he might find concerning the ransacking of the place while her mother slept? Now go into the restroom and wash your face."

For once, I did as he asked. It didn't take long, since I had no comb for my stray, wiry hair and no makeup in my backpack. I smoothed my hair and left it at that.

Blake was waiting at the door, twirling his hat on his finger.

When we went outside, the sky was overcast and gray. Rain was coming down in buckets, and in the distance, thunder rumbled. "God is crying over Rosa Leigh, too," I said, and a sob took away my breath.

Chapter 23

We drove in and out of rain all the way to the hospital. In some areas, the water rolled down the ditch lines, and in others, the pavement was only damp. A half hour later, Blake pulled up to the main entrance, and the valet sprinted out with a ticket. We hurried inside, and the receptionist directed us to the fifth floor waiting area where Janene was the only occupant. As soon as I entered the room, she hurried to me.

"I'm so glad to see you. She's been in recovery a long time, and they should be moving her to her room soon. The surgery went well. They found three malignant tumors on the left, rather than the two they thought there were. One was at nine o'clock, one at six and one at twelve. They took out ten lymph nodes, seven were cancerous."

She turned and went back to the sofa. Blake and I followed her. She picked up a folded newspaper and whacked me on the arm. "What were you thinking?! This doesn't look good for our agency. Snooping in a ninety-two-year-old person's house like a little kid doesn't make good press."

I sat in a chair across from her. "Don't worry. The little rinky-dinky newspaper here doesn't have reporters. They rely on the public to supply information. I don't see Ms. Overstreet, or Danita, taking the time to write up the information and then submit it. And besides, we don't care. We have only one job here, and ransacking a house isn't going to make the national news. Therefore, no one in Florida will know a thing about it."

Blake stepped toward me. "You are not stupid. So, stop acting as if you are. With the social access people have today, you have no clue who this story might reach." He grabbed his hat off his knee, rose and started for the door.

A tall, skinny female nurse entered, blocked his way and said, "Ms. Adams is in her room, and if you'll follow me, I'll take you there."

Janene, Blake and I followed her. We walked down a long L-shaped hall. Smells of strong antiseptic lingered in the air. Voices floated from each room, some from television shows and others from visitors. We turned left at the end of the hall and made another left into the first room on the corner. Rosa Leigh smiled at us from her bed.

I rushed to her side. "Are you in pain?"

She shook her head and opened her arms for me. "Crazy old friend. I ought to divorce you."

"You can't divorce friends," I said. "You're stuck with me."

We hugged, and I stepped aside for Janene. Rosa Leigh motioned for me to sit in a chair close to her bed, so I did.

"I have to stay the night, but I need a ride tomorrow."

I leaned forward. "You know I'll be here."

She stared deep into my eyes. "Are you sure you can stop looking for the skull and be here by 9:00?" Rosa Leigh asked and smiled, tilting her head to one side. "Stop being angry with yourself. Until the doctor's office called me, I didn't know I was having surgery today. If you'd known in time, I know you would have been there. I'm not upset with you because Janene had to bring me to the hospital. I'm angry with you because you invaded someone's privacy. How would you feel if someone searched through your belongings without permission?"

Guilt churned my stomach, and I squirmed, pulling my eyes away from my friend. "I got my priorities in the wrong place, Rosa Leigh. I won't let you and Blake down again." I lowered my head.

A hand brushed my forearm, and Blake's muscular scent filled the air. My body tingled. I looked up, and the glimmer in his eyes reminded me of our younger days. An unfortunate clanging sound in the hall caused me to tear my eyes away from his sizzling blue ones. A short lady walked into the room with a food tray, placed it on the bedside table and left.

"Blake, will you raise the head of my bed?" Rosa Leigh asked. He did, and she pushed herself up a little taller. "Thank you."

She said grace aloud and glanced at me. "Why don't you go home and feed Simon. By the time you drive there, it will be past his dinner time."

"Okay. I will," I said, "and I'll eat something myself before he gets his evening walk."

Janene stood. "I need to go, too. It will be dark soon, and I don't want to be on these crooked roads alone." She looked at me. "There's no need for Blake to drive you home, Ives. You can ride with me."

"It's no trouble," Blake said. "In fact, I'll feel relieved when I get her inside the house and know she's out of trouble."

I kissed Rosa Leigh's cheek. "Good night. I'll see you in the morning."

Outside, the overcast sky made everything gloomy and gray. The air was thick with precipitation and heat. Blake's car arrived first, and the three of us waited in silence for the valet to bring Janene's. When her red rental arrived, she slid beneath the steering wheel and followed us out of the parking area. We left the bright lights of the city, and drove into the dark countryside. Thinking about walking Simon alone tonight, I shivered. I felt Blake's eyes on me and hazarded a look, but I couldn't read his face.

"If you want to walk Simon tonight, I suggest we do it when we reach Rosa Leigh's, so you won't have to walk alone. Copperhead Ridge isn't the safe place you once lived in," he said.

"How did you do that?" I asked.

"Do what?"

"Read my mind."

His booming laugh filled the car. "I have no paranormal power. I simply remembered you're afraid of the dark."

"I am not."

He chuckled. "You always saw long bony fingers coming at you from the trees and ghosts lurking in the shadows."

"I'm touched you remember so much about me, but I always saw myself as the bravest of our group."

The corner of his mouth curled up, and when he glanced my way, the dashboard lights flickered in his eyes.

"You were in the daytime. You were the risk-taker and still are. Remember the time you talked all of us into diving off the cliff into the stream at Carter Caves?"

"I wouldn't call it a risk-taking adventure. Everyone jumped from a small boulder, ten feet above the water."

"The adults dove from there. We were how old? Eight or nine?"

I smiled and hitched my chin. "No one got hurt."

"Didn't they? We had to go under the water to search for John Tolssin. It was the last time he went near water."

A small chill swept across my neck. "A stupid thing for us to do. We could have all drowned."

Blake patted my arm. "We weren't. And most of the challenges you gave us were good for us."

We chatted about teenage memories until he turned into Rosa Leigh's drive. Janene coasted beside the cruiser and stopped. She slid out, waved and let herself into the house.

Blake gazed at the sky. "Go get Simon. The clouds are heavy, but we'll create our own stars." Laughing, he jogged around the car and opened my door.

The look in his eyes sent a tingle through me. He bent and offered me his lips. I touched mine to his, and forty years disappeared. I was eighteen again, and every hormone in my body was alive.

"Don't forget your life's in Florida," he said. "You need to ask yourself if you're ready for what we're doing."

Chapter 24

The next morning, I was in Rosa Leigh's room before 9:00 A.M., as promised. She was dressed and sitting on the side of the bed awaiting her chariot…a wheelchair.

I kissed her cheek. "You were so sure I'd be here on time you ordered your transport?"

She smiled and nodded. "You have always been a friend I could depend on."

Within seconds, a nurse entered the room. "Your ride is right on time, Me Lady. You will be home in time for tea and scones."

Rosa Leigh chuckled, and her delightful laugh made me smile. "Not unless Ives stops to buy both."

And we all laughed.

The nurse looked at me. "You can pull the car to the entrance. We'll be waiting there for you."

"Okay." I rushed from the room and maneuvered my way through the hospital employees and visitors. By the time I arrived at the entrance with our car, the nurse had Rosa Leigh outside.

Suddenly, a car pulled into the space in front of us, almost hitting me. The driver struggled out, gave me a nasty look and walked to a woman standing next to a frail man in a wheelchair. In a loud voice, he swore and pointed to me, still in the driver's seat of my car. "Some people always think of themselves first. You'd think she'd pull down farther, so I could drive closer to the curb for you."

The nurse and Rosa Leigh gave him the devil's stare, but neither said a word. By the time the door opened for the nurse to help my friend into the car, I was livid. "Hey you, Numbskull! This pick-up space is for all patients who are going home."

Rosa Leigh tried to shush me, but I wasn't willing to let it go. "And your car, nor the three of you, were in sight when I drove to the curb."

The nurse said, "Goodbye, Ms. Adams, and good luck." She whirled the chair around and hustled through the double doors.

The arrogant driver's lips curled into a snarl, and he yelled, "You have to wait until we're loaded because I've now blocked you in." He grabbed the wheelchair and pushed it off the curb. The elderly man's head bobbed from side-to-side.

I wanted to kick the driver's behind, but for Rosa Leigh's sake, I didn't say a word as the maniac loaded his passenger. The older woman with him walked in front of our car, smiled at us and then stuck out her tongue. We burst into hysterical laughter, until tears streamed down our cheeks.

The driver rolled the chair to the back of the car, popped his trunk and heaved it into the car. He took out a white sign, faced us and placed the magnetized sign on his trunk.

It read "Handicapped Driving Service". We broke into uncontrollable laughter again, and he gave us the finger.

Rosa Leigh looked at me. "Well, he's definitely the handicapped one."

I laughed until I hiccupped.

The driver lumbered to the front of his car, got in and started the engine. His back-up lights turned on. I glanced in my rearview mirror. There was a line of vehicles behind us waiting their turn. I couldn't back out of the idiot's way. His eyes shifted to his rear mirror. He eased the car over the curb, barely missing the pillar holding up the entrance's roof, and put it into reverse again.

Rosa Leigh shrieked, "Brace yourself!"

After about three attempts at moving the car forward and back, he drove into the street and sped away.

Rosa Leigh giggled and said, "It's a gorgeous day, no clouds, seventy-five degrees." She rolled down her window. "And I want to feel the wind on my face."

Soon, we were out of the city and away from the smell of gasoline, diesel fuel and mingled odors of foods. The air blowing in through the window felt cooler than seventy-five, but terrific all the same. I inhaled the wonderful fragrance of pine rushing in.

Every mile or two, there was a gap in the trees leading back to houses nestled at the foot of the mountain. The long driveways of dirt and gravel were lined with weeds and filled with potholes.

When oncoming vehicles passed us, the wind shivered the leaves creating a silver sheen, and behind the trees, the mountain stood tall. We passed the cliffs running along Copperhead Ridge and pulled into Rosa Leigh's drive.

When I turned off the engine off, I said, "I know you don't want me coddling you, but you're not supposed to lift over five pounds. Straining to open the door might cause you pain. I'll do that for you."

Inside, Simon rose from his spot beside the front door. "Stay down," Rosa Leigh warned him, and bent enough to give him a hug. The two made their way through the narrow hall to the dining room.

I dropped her overnight bag beside the door in the foyer and walked near her and Simon into her dining area. "Can I fix you a sandwich?"

She shook her head. "I want to sit by the window in my recliner, read a good book and glance out to watch the fish jump in the lake."

A door opened down the hallway, and we turned as Janene came into the dining room. "You look great! Your cheeks are rosy, your eyes are sparkly, and you're smiling. What a woman!"

Rosa Leigh lifted her hands. "I have two choices. I can curl up and feel sorry for myself or put one foot in front of the other and go on with life. Besides, no one wants to be around a person who moans and groans over every little pain." She sat in the recliner by the French doors and lifted the lever. Simon stretched out on the floor beside her. She pointed at Janene. "You hurry and finish your novel. I want to be the first to read it."

Janene gave a military hand to her forehead. "I have thirty thousand words. And back to work I go." She walked the few steps towards the hall and turned back around. "I'm glad you're home, Rosa Leigh," she said and disappeared.

I called down the hall after her, "A whole week and you only have thirty thousand words?"

Janene waved over her shoulder. "It takes time to paint settings and create plots with words." She closed the door to her wing.

I handed Rosa Leigh her book from the stand by the chair. "Do you have everything you need?"

She nodded.

"I'm going to walk Simon now," I said. "We won't be gone long."

She spread a lap quilt across her legs. "Take your time. I'll probably be asleep within the first ten pages. My room was across from the nurse's station, and every time I dozed, someone would drop something or laugh."

I strolled across the dining room to the kitchen door. "Let's go for a walk."

Simon rose to his feet and came to me. Circling the house, we walked down the drive and turned toward the cemetery. He loped ahead.

With no shade, the direct sun felt more like ninety degrees, and burned my skin through my blouse. Simon waited for me at the cemetery gate. I yelled for him and turned to go home, but he raced across the road, bounded around the pond and stood at the path leading to the Overstreet property.

"We're not going into the woods today. Come back here," I said and sat on the bench, while he stood at the path, staring over his shoulder. "You better take your swim. I'm not staying long."

Simon stayed where he was, waiting for me to join him. I ignored him, until my tongue began to stick to the roof of my mouth. I'd left in such a hurry, I'd forgotten to bring water. "Come on. I need a drink."

He didn't budge, and when I walked towards the woods, he disappeared through the bushes. I checked the pathway as far as I could see, but I didn't see him. "Simon, come here!"

When he didn't show, I yelled again, but he still didn't come.

I do have a reason to go after him. But my thinking changed when images of my time in the small jail cell flitted before my eyes.

I called his name again, but he didn't bark or appear. I stepped beneath the canopy of leaves and inched forward a few steps. I didn't want to disappoint Blake by disobeying the restraining order. I called the dog again, but he still didn't come.

Surely, Danita wouldn't press charges if I explain I was chasing Simon.

I crept forward a few steps and stopped. *She'll have me arrested.*

I searched for my cell phone and remembered it was in my purse. *I can't call Janene to follow him, and for all I know, I'm standing on the Overstreet property now.*

"I'm going home, Simon!" I yelled one more time.

I ran from the woods, circled the pond like a drunk woman and forced myself onto the dusty gravel road. *Why does it have to be difficult to do the right thing?* I walked home alone, and interrupted Janene.

After I explained Simon's trip into the trees, and probably to the Overstreet property, she changed into long pants and tennis shoes. But before she needed to help me, Simon scratched at the back door. Aggravated with him, I let him in and went into my bedroom to watch the latest hurricane update.

The weatherman pointed at the map. "The hurricane is downgraded to Level 1 as it passes over land. It's leaving devastation behind, though. People are without electricity. Nursing homes are evacuating residents to other areas with electricity. One nursing facility had two deaths from the heat last night and more residents are in critical condition." He continued to show the wind direction. It was south and in a direct line with Palmetto. I called my friend in Florida.

"Did you go to the shelter?" I asked as soon as she answered.

"No, but it's the scariest thing I've endured, and it's only side winds. I'll leave next time."

"Wouldn't Melvin go to a safe place?"

"By the time he agreed to leave, the shelters were already full. He'd wanted to wait until the storm was closer. It made me angry, and so when he decided he wanted to go, I refused."

I scratched my head. "You better thank God for keeping you safe. Was there damage in our complex?"

She sighed. "You're lucky. Your place only lost the carport. Others have roofs off and lanais destroyed. When I saw all the damage, it scared me even worse than the storm roaring overhead last night, and I didn't sleep a wink."

"Serves you right, silly bugger. I'm sure Janene will want to catch the first flight home."

Music blared through the line. "Melvin, turn the television down. I can't hear." She waited until the sound lowered. "Tell her there's no need. There's no electricity in Florida, and the Skyway Bridge is closed until further notice. They're saying it might be days before electricity is restored. Stay put until they open the bridge. Besides, most of the flights into Florida are canceled. I'll call as soon as the bridge opens, and you have lights."

"Thank you and take care of yourself. I don't know what I'd do if anything happened to you," I said and told her goodbye.

Standing alone in the room waiting for Janene, I considered the situation in Florida and the one I was in here. *Rosa Leigh needs me more. She sent for me. And not to find the stupid skull. She's going to need a driver for the trips to chemo and radiation.* I gazed out across the lake. *Any one of her friends can take her, but she asked me to be*

here. How will I take care of the mangled carport, though?
The manager won't let the debris lay long. I wrung my
hands.

Chapter 25

Simon scratching at the back door was a pleasant distraction from my worries. "You're not going outside again." I glanced out to see why he was anxious to get out and saw a rabbit playing in the grass near the lake.

Rosa Leigh called from the dining area, wanting to know what the dog was carrying on about. I told her about the furry friend, and she mumbled. The only words I heard were "disgusting habit."

I opened the refrigerator door and called over my shoulder, "I think I'll cook dinner."

Janene walked into the kitchen asking, "What's Ives done now?"

I set out a package of steaks and said, "You are uninvited to dinner."

She bowed as if I were royalty. "Please accept my humble apologies. It's been . . ."

She paused, and her eyes twinkled with mischief. "How long has it been since I've eaten one of your cooked dinners?" She snapped her fingers. "Oh, now I remember. Never! Are we having cake for the main course, perhaps pie and cupcakes for sides and your famous peanut butter fudge for dessert?"

I grinned. "You have a smart mouth. I don't like to cook, but I know how. Can you say the same?"

She giggled. "If TV dinners, Hamburger Helper and boxed mac and cheese count, yes, I can."

"What are we having?" Rosa Leigh asked, still in her favorite chair in the dining room.

I walked to the door where I can see her. "What do you want?"

She rolled her eyes towards the ceiling, thinking. "Fix your famous chicken and dumplings, green beans, ripe tomatoes and chocolate cake."

I returned the steaks to the refrigerator and said, "I'll make a grocery run."

When I walked from kitchen into the dining room to the hall to get my purse and keys, Rosa Leigh stopped me.

"Chicken and dumplings have too many calories. Let's have your baked chicken and dressing instead."

"No potatoes?"

She shook her head. "The dressing will be enough carbs with the cake. Janene can work on her book awhile more, though. I plan to take a nap, and I might sleep until dinner. If I do, wake me."

As I continued down the hall to my room, I said over my shoulder, "Janene will be here if you need anything." I snatched my purse off the hook on the inside of the door, walked back down the hall and stood near her chair. "Do you mind if I invite Blake? I owe the man my life for keeping me out of jail."

She held my hand and smiled up at me. "How do you ever repay someone for your freedom?"

Janene piped up, "With the sparks flying between the two, she'll be married to him before I can take her home."

I felt a fluttering in my stomach, the way it used to be at the mere mention of his name. "One dinner does not make a marriage, Ladies," I said and scurried out the door, followed by Simon. "You won't behave for me, so I can't take you into town. Go back around to your day spot on the porch, and don't you dare go into the lake or kill a helpless animal."

As I drove away, he stood at the corner of the house, looking pitiful.

* * *

I stopped at the jail first. Blake was sitting at his desk doing paperwork. He motioned me to the chair in front of him. "Is Rosa Leigh home?"

I nodded. "She's probably sleeping like a baby right now since the hospital noise kept her awake last night."

He leaned back in his chair and looked at me. "What brings you into Three Pines?"

"Grocery shopping for dinner. Would you like to come?"

He looked to his right to the empty jail cell. "This place is empty, but is Rosa Leigh up for visitors this soon?"

"She said you could come." I smiled. "You've always had a spot in her heart."

A grin spread across his face, and his blue eyes sparkled. "Is this her idea?"

I scooted my bottom back in the chair. "Dinner is a thank you for keeping me from being arrested. I let Rosa Leigh decide the menu, though. Do you want to know what we're having before you decide?"

He leaned forward and placed his arms on the desk. "No. I will love spending my evening with three beautiful women. Food will not be important."

I slapped my thighs and said, "All righty. I'll see you around 6:00." As I walked out the door, I gave a wave over my shoulder. There was that fluttering in my stomach again and an excitement I hadn't felt in years.

I bought the groceries and drove home from town in record time. The rest of the afternoon, I putzed around, breaking fresh green beans, setting the table, anything I could do to use up my restless energy.

Around 4:00, I took a shower, put on my sea foam-colored blouse and a pair of white pants. The blue-green close to my face highlighted my gray eyes and white hair. I sponged on foundation, brushed some rose blush on my cheeks and put on a pair of sea glass earrings the color of my blouse. I looked at myself in the long mirror. "You look good for a sixty-two-year-old. You worked hard, ate healthy and exercised to keep the weight off. One hundred and twenty pounds looks great on your five-foot, four-inch frame."

I turned to see my back side, and whispered, "My eyelids droop, my boobs sag, and my bottom has dropped, but like I told my partners, I still catch the men's eyes." I giggled at my own absurdity. "But the men can no longer turn their heads. They turn their whole body." I laughed all the way into the kitchen.

Rosa Leigh liked dressing made from stale bread, but I couldn't find any. So, I'd bought a bag of flavored croutons and added sage, onions and chicken broth for flavor.

I inserted butter beneath the skin on the chicken breast to moisten it, filled the cavity with the dressing and placed the remainder in the baking pan with the bird. She didn't like it baked separately. After I put my green beans in the pressure cooker with three strips of bacon and two cups of water, I set a timer so they could cook and depressurize while the meat baked.

Rosa Leigh had said she didn't want potatoes, but I baked sweet potatoes while the meat was cooking. They were lower in carbs, so that should make her happy. We could put butter, brown sugar and cinnamon on them, just like we liked them. Rosa Leigh didn't have to eat them, but Blake liked a potato with his meal. I scrubbed them, wrapped them in aluminum foil, popped them into the oven and glance at the clock. It was 5:00, and the food would be ready on time.

I was on a bar stool reviewing the food list and heard someone in the hall. It was Janene. "Something smells yummy. What are we having?"

I named the dishes, and she raised one eyebrow. "No dessert from the baking queen of Shimmering Lake in Florida?"

A sick feeling came over me. "Good grief! How could I forget?"

She opened the oven and sniffed. "Oh, my goodness. You're dressing smells like my mom's. I love it." She turned. "You know, dessert is Rosa Leigh's most important part of the meal."

Biting my upper lip, I thought of a quick dessert. "I've got it! Both Rosa Leigh and Blake love chocolate. I'll mix up a microwave chocolate cake with a chocolate sauce."

I hurried to the refrigerator, opened the freezer compartment and blew out a long breath. "Great! There's the quart of French Vanilla ice cream I brought home last week."

Janene climbed up on a stool. "Sounds delicious."

I glanced at her. "Done writing for the day?"

She placed her arms on the counter and propped her chin in one hand. "I'm going to take a shower and dress for dinner in a minute. I'm deciding if I want a cup of tea or a glass of water."

As I listened to her chatter about plot decision after plot decision, I took out two mixing bowls, cocoa, sugar, butter, vanilla, milk and walnuts and began measuring my dry ingredients. *Topped with ice cream, it'll make a decadent dessert. They'll think I've slaved all day.*

The clock on the oven buzzed as the doorbell rang. Janene darted through the hall to her wing to get ready.

When I opened the door, Blake handed me a bud vase with a single rose. "Is pink still your favorite rose?"

The butterflies in my stomach hadn't aged a bit. They were as active as when I was in my teens. I took the flower and smiled till I didn't think I could smile any bigger.

"The lady at the shop made the pink ribbon for you," he said, his eyes shimmering.

I kept smiling because I just couldn't stop and said, "No one's given me flowers in . . ."

I paused to think and to calm the rascals going crazy in my stomach. "I guess since my husband died. Thank you." I motioned for him to enter.

He stepped into the foyer. "I tend to arrive too soon."

I nudged him towards the kitchen. "Absolutely not. It'll give us more time to catch up. The chicken needs to rest a few minutes to cool before I cut it." I walked to the hallway with Blake following me, hoping I looked great to him from that viewpoint. "Hurry up, ladies, while dinner is hot. Can I fix you a drink, Blake?"

He shook his head and sat on a stool. "Do I smell sage and onions?"

"You do. Rosa Leigh requested baked chicken and dressing."

He stood and came up close beside me, so near I felt his body heat. "And you remember those are two of my all-time favorite foods, right?"

You smell divine. Clean and musky and masculine. And you wore my favorite colors on you, aqua shirt and beige slacks. This evening could not be more perfect.

I rolled my eyes. "It's my way of apologizing for the aggravation I caused you over the Overstreet incident."

Disappointment spread across his face, and he strolled to the dining room French doors and stared out across the lake. "I was hoping dinner was because you want to spend time with me." He gazed my way and then back to the lake. "What we would have given for a body of water like this lake when we were in high school."

"We had lots of fun at the reservoir, didn't we?" I said, feeling terrible that I'd upset him.

Surely, he knew I was feeling the same things about us that he was?

He returned to the kitchen. "But it was public."

As I sat the beautiful rose on the counter, I grabbed an oven mitt and took out the chicken, potatoes and the green bean casserole to cool. A door opened in the hall. Rosa Leigh walked into the room holding herself up against the wall.

"Ives, we will dine with the best-looking man in Kentucky tonight," she said.

"I'd give you a hug, Blake, but . . ." She studied her flat chest area. "I'm still too sore."

He took her hands and kissed her cheek. "I hope the pain is minimal."

"It is. And I believe when I accept my new normal, I'll be happy I did it. I couldn't have made the decision without your advice, though." She sat in a chair at the dining room table. "I will forever be indebted to you, guy friend. Your shoulders are as broad as I remember them to be. If you hadn't been head-over-heels in love with Ives back then, I would've snatched you up." She laughed.

I dished up the food, and as soon as Blake saw me take two dishes to the table, he brought the others.

"Janene!" Rosa Leigh yelled down the hall and shushed us, waiting on a response. After a few seconds, she said, "There's no sound coming from her room. Go hurry the woman."

As I neared her room, Janene sauntered out. The fragrance of her citrus body wash filled the narrow space. She put up her hands and brushed past me. "I know. Next time I'll shower and dress earlier."

Everyone was seated, except me. I was about to sit when Simon whined. "Aww, poor baby. I forgot to walk you this afternoon. You lie down, and I'll take you later."

He walked to his spot by the door and gave me a pitiful look. "Hey, give me credit. I fed you before I cooked." He laid down, stretched his strawberry colored paws out in front of him and rested his head on them. I sat down next to Blake.

Rosa Leigh placed her elbows on the table and teepeed her hands. "I'll say grace. It's been over five years since Ives has cooked anything but desserts. That itself deserves a prayer of gratitude."

Everyone burst out laughing, and when her prayer was done, Rosa Leigh began describing the first of the hilarious stunts we'd survived during our teens.

When we finished my decadent dessert, Janene said, "I have enough material to write another book."

Blake pointed a finger at her. "Don't you dare! I have a sparkling reputation, and if you print some of these stories, the local teens won't respect me."

"I use a composite of a number of people to develop my characters. If I write the setting somewhere other than Kentucky, no one will recognize you," she assured him and winked.

Simon whined, stood and shook all over.

I gazed out the window. "It's dark outside." I went to him and smoothed his back. "But, you've been a good dog. So, come on, let's go," I said and opened the back door.

Blake pushed back his chair and followed me. "Not without me, you don't."

I fluttered my eyelashes. "Why, Sheriff, if someone got me, come daylight, they would let me go."

He smiled and nudged me out the door. "What if it's not human?"

Chapter 26

I thought about Blake's comment and shuddered. Kentucky didn't have crocodiles, alligators or pythons, but the copperheads and rattlesnakes were just as deadly.

Simon trotted ahead as Blake and I walked out the driveway and turned the opposite way of the cemetery.

Blake bumped my shoulder and pointed up. "Isn't it a beautiful sight?"

"I'd forgotten how gorgeous the sky is in the country, away from the city lights."

Brilliant stars peppered the sky as far as you could see. The half-moon was a golden yellow and gave enough light to see the road without using our flashlight. We walked without talking.

I breathed in the pine fragrance of the trees lining one side of the pavement. An owl called from the other side where hickory, maple and elm grew. The other birds and animals were quiet.

Blake closed the distance between us. "May I hold your hand?"

As I took his hand, memories flooded my brain of starlit nights and walks talking about our future. Neither of us had considered going forward without the other. And here we were forty-four years later, trying to figure it out again.

He squeezed my hand gently, bringing me back to the moment. "Did you think about me?" He asked.

I nodded then realized he couldn't see that in the dark. "When you refused to leave this area, my heart broke. From our first date, you knew I didn't plan to stay around here. I was angry with you, and I doubt there was a day that passed, until I met my husband, that I didn't wonder if you'd found someone else. Did you think you could keep me here?"

He looked at me. "I believed our love was strong enough that we'd work things out. I knew I never wanted to leave here permanently. You knew I wanted to be in law enforcement, all along. Truly, I thought once you went to college and got your fill of the city, you'd be ready to return and marry me." He stopped and faced me. "I waited for you. And the day you were married, my heart broke. But I think both of us had a good life. Don't you?"

I thought about what he'd said as we strolled behind Simon. "I didn't think I'd find anyone I loved as much as you, but I did. And as we built our life together, you faded from my life." I chuckled. "Seven children kept me hopping."

"I bet they're all wonderful and didn't give you an ounce of trouble."

"They were—"

Rustling in the trees stopped me cold.

Simon stopped, too, and turned to the woods and growled.

Blake froze. "Ssshh."

He turned to his right to the thrashing in the underbrush and danced the flashlight through the leaves. "Something's in there." He stepped toward the noise.

I clutched his hand so tight, it hurt mine. "No, you don't, Mister," I whispered. "You're not leaving me, and I'm not venturing in there."

He tugged my hand, and we walked on. "It's probably a rodent."

Neither of us talked. We were too busy listening. We hadn't gone far when the rustling began again. As soon as we stopped, it stopped. We took steps. And, it moved.

Fear prickled my flesh.

I leaned close to Blake and said as quietly as I could, "Let's go back. Simon's walked enough." I bent down and whispered, "Come on, Simon. Let's go home."

Unlike his normal bravado, he snuggled close to me. The three of us were soon fast-walking. The thing in the bushes, though, was keeping up with us. By the time we reached the drive, we were loping. As the mysterious being gained on us, I sprinted down around the house and darted in the back door. Simon ran in next, followed by Blake.

Hearing our commotion, the women raced into the kitchen from the living room. Rosa Leigh's eyes were wide with fear. "What on earth happened?! You two are white."

I gulped a big breath. "I think we were being stalked by a ghost."

Janene cupped her hands over her mouth. "There's no such thing as ghosts," she said, her words coming out muffled.

Simon rubbed against Rosa Leigh's leg, and she bent to pet him. "I've never seen one, but this dog is trembling, and he's not afraid of anything."

Blake turned from the door glass, where he'd been looking out. "There's no sign of anything out there. I'm sure it was a large, nosy animal. Though Simon's brave in the daylight, Ladies, it doesn't mean he's not afraid of the dark. He's not accustomed to being out at night, is he, Rosa Leigh?"

She rolled her eyes upward, thinking. "Actually, I don't remember ever letting him out after dark."

Janene's hands dropped. "Whew. I like those deductive skills, Sir. It makes sense to me."

Blake smiled. "I need to be going." He looked at me. "Thank you for the delicious dinner. I'll call you soon and take you out for a lovely meal, and we can finish our conversation."

"Sounds good to me," I said, and as he disappeared in the dark, I closed the door.

"Ives can tell us about that talk over a cup of coffee and more cake," Rosa Leigh said, walking to the pot.

Janene took her arm and re-routed her to her chair beside the French doors. "I'll brew you a cup and bring you more cake. You're to be resting."

I rubbed the prickly bumps on my arms. "I won't sleep a wink if I drink caffeine. I don't kiss and tell anyway, Rosa Leigh."

She pointed to the chairs at the table. "Sit, and we'll talk awhile then about old times while I drink mine. Nothing keeps me awake."

"How is your pain level?" I asked.

"I'm sore, but the hospital wrapped me tight. The only things I need to pay attention to at the present are the drain tubes at each side. Is tomorrow the day the nurse will come to change the bandages?"

"I believe so," I said and sat at the table.

When Janene brought her coffee and cake, the two of us talked and Janene listened until midnight when she decided she needed sleep. "I won't be alert enough to write tomorrow if I don't go to bed. I could sit all night and listen to you two, but I will say goodnight."

I took Rosa Leigh's dishes to the sink, rinsed and stack them in the dishwasher. Returning to where she was seated, I said, "Let's go, girlfriend, I'll help you put on your pjs."

She reached a hand to me, and Simon walked ahead, settling into his spot at the foot of her bed. Once I had her snug, I went to my room and fell asleep to the sounds of crickets and croaking frogs.

Sometime in the wee hours, I sat straight up and stared into the blackness, not knowing what had awoken me. As my eyes adjusted, the dark shape of the chest, dressing table and the open door took form. A mound of something, or someone, was silhouetted in my doorway by the hall nightlight.

My stomach flipflopped.

A loud clang startled me.

I jumped out of bed, and the mound ran towards me.

I screamed.

Simon yipped.

"You scared me, crazy dog!"

A louder clang vibrated through the night air. Simon barked and trotted into the living room.

Janene's door opened, and she ran to my room. Then, Rosa Leigh's door opened. She's carrying a baseball bat in one hand and her 9mm in the other hand.

I raced to the large living room window, lifted the drape and peeked out. The security lamp lit the front yard.

Nothing was visible.

I slid to the other side and looked that direction. No human or animal was on the drive. I rushed to the dining area where Simon barked ferociously at the French doors. Rosa Leigh stood to one side of the doors and Janene was on the other, peeking through the slats of the closed vertical blinds.

I whispered, "Do you see anything?"

Rosa Leigh waved me closer. I tapped her shoulder and edged in to push a slat of the blind to the side. The house blocked the front security light, but the moon and stars cast enough light to see two silhouettes trying to break into the tool shed where Rosa Leigh kept her zero-turn lawn mower. A third person was tinkering with one of the two jet skis at the dock.

Rosa Leigh snatched her cell phone off the reading table and punched in 9-1-1. She whispered her request and finished with, "Hurry, please!"

We continued to watch as the two figures hit the lock with a sledgehammer. The other one jogged from the dock to the shed. Their muted voices echoed through the heavy air. One guy crept to the kitchen door. The knob rattled. The sound of metal scraping metal echoed through the room.

The front door groaned.

I whirled around.

A shadow stood in the front doorway.

"If you live in this area, you know I hit what I aim at," Rosa Leigh yelled. "If not, you will because the next bullet has your name on it."

Her arm raised.

A spark flashed.

A loud boom reverberated into the night.

Outside, footsteps thumped by the house towards the front, seeking an escape.

An engine revved in the road.

I turned to the French door and peeked out in time to see a shadow of a rickety truck roll up to the building. A light went on inside the cab. Two robbers jumped in, and the door slammed. The truck sped out of the drive and headed towards town.

Janene and I yanked and tugged each other's pajama tops, trying to beat the other into the living room. I folded the drape back, crawled beneath it and watched the truck burn rubber. When the taillights of the rattle trap disappeared, I clawed my way out and found myself in an empty room. I ran through the foyer to the kitchen.

Rosa Leigh was in the backyard, dancing the flashlight beam over the shed, and Janene was almost glued to her side. They searched around the building and returned to the door. I ran to where they were standing.

"Dang! When did you become a sharpshooter?" I asked Rosa Leigh.

Rosa Leigh shined the light in my eyes, blinding me. "I took weeks of training." She closed the door, put the lever back over the large steeple-like holder and inserted the broken prong. "Maybe it'll fool burglars who come calling, but it won't keep them out. I'll replace the lock tomorrow."

As we walked back to the house, sirens trilled in the distance.

Janene entered the kitchen, grumbling, "Ives, you've put all of us in danger looking for that skull."

Rosa Leigh chimed in, "I told her to stop. I used the cave and skull to motivate her to be with me through my surgery." She stared at me. "And stay with me during my treatments. However, I don't believe these had anything to do with the cave or skull. I think they came to steal tools and any other item they could load easily to sell for drug money."

As I closed the door, I said, "I agree. It was druggies."

If it was the men who left me in the cave, I think they wouldn't have bothered with the shed. They would have broken in the house and . . .

I trembled.

Who knows what they would have done to my friends and me?

Chapter 27

Twenty minutes after the robbers hightailed it out of Rosa Leigh's driveway, Blake's cruiser screeched to a stop, siren screaming. He rushed to the front door, and I hurried to open it to prevent him from worrying.

He inquired about our well-being and had us tell him about the events. After he jotted notes in a spiral notepad, he jammed it into his front shirt pocket, and said to me, "Show me the damage to the shed and pool house." He turned to Rosa Leigh and said, "Please stay seated and rest. I know the attempted burglary terrified you."

As we walked out the back to the two buildings I asked, "Do all law enforcement people carry tiny spiral pads to take notes?"

Blake chuckled. "Some carry larger ones. Why?"

"The policemen in Palmetto and Bradenton use the smaller size. I thought it might be a standard regulation," I said and pointed to the broken shed lock, making a mental note to get myself a tablet.

He leaned over and shined his flashlight on the latch. "We're required to keep a log, or notes. It's easier for me to carry one small enough to keep in my pocket. Otherwise, I'd have to return to the car for the one I also leave on the seat or under the visor. Did anyone handle the lock?"

"Rosa Leigh did."

"Take me to the pool house. I'll dust for prints, but if the men aren't in the data base, it won't do much good, except it will rule out Rosa Leigh's."

We walked to the far end of the pool. "This building is never locked," I said. "They went for the jet skis, but they didn't have a key."

"I think it was the locals who need money for drugs," Blake said. "They must have taken a side road, because I didn't pass any cars coming here."

As we returned to the house I said, "I'm assuming they live nearby."

He opened the door for me, "Maybe, or maybe not. There's an intricate network of roads leading through the county."

Inside, Blake addressed Rosa Leigh. "You'd better replace the locks tomorrow. If they return, do what you did tonight. Call 9-1-1 first and make certain where each robber is before you open the door to fire. If they cover both doors, fire the gun from the furthest window. The sound usually scares them off. In the meantime, try to rest."

To me, he said, "I'll see you tomorrow evening around 5:30."

I nodded and closed the door behind him. The clock chimed 2:00 A.M., and Rosa Leigh, Janene and Simon went to bed.

I was too wired to sleep, however, and settled in the living room to watch the Weather Channel. The devastation in Florida took away my breath. The videos of the aftermath from the hurricane were heartbreaking. It nearly destroyed the Caribbean Islands, and the weather specialist said it would take years to rebuild Key West. It was a miracle there were no fatalities.

Baking always relieved stress for me, and I'd stocked Rosa Leigh's kitchen with a few things. I looked for the ingredients to make cinnamon rolls. To me, nothing smelled better than the aroma of warm yeast and cinnamon. The batch made enough for three people to make hogs of themselves and de-stress, and perhaps leave one or two for Blake.

When they were in the oven, I called my friend Gwendalyn, an early riser. I held my breath, praying she had her cell charged and on, and when she said hello, I sighed relief.

"We have electricity in spots," she told me, "but certain grids in the complex still do not. Some of the neighbors are freezing ice to give to people for their freezers. A coffee angel arrived here on a golf cart a few minutes ago. She's still in her pajamas, but she's knocking on all doors serving anyone who wants some. I've never had a better tasting cup. How is your friend?"

After I told her how Rosa Leigh was doing medically, she told me she couldn't talk long, due to her low battery. "It's good to know you both are doing well. Stay safe and call me with updates."

I disconnected and turned to feet slapping against the wood floor in the hallway.

Rosa Leigh entered the kitchen, filled a mug with coffee and climbed on a bar stool. "You made your mother's cinnamon rolls."

"I did," I said, peeking inside the oven.

The buns were a golden brown, and perfect. I placed them on top of the stove to cool.

Rosa Leigh sipped her brew while I mixed up a pastry glaze. As I spread it on the tops, the door at the end of the hall opened and then slammed.

"I smell cinnamon rolls," Janene called as she scrambled toward the kitchen.

I puffed a lock of hair off my forehead. "In the future, if I need to, I'll know how to wake the two of you early."

I finished frosting the buns and took three plates from the cupboard. While I placed breakfast on the plates, Rosa Leigh wiggled on the stool, complaining that I was torturing her.

"I want two," Janene said and flipped her hair over her shoulder. "I'll exercise later."

Rosa Leigh took a bite and moaned. "We will have plenty of physical activity today. We're going to see a play in Columbus. Jersey Donovan will be riding with us."

Rosa Leigh had evidently scheduled this event before her diagnosis and had forgotten to cancel. "Rosa Leigh, the doctor told you not to drive until your staples are out. Are you strong enough to go to an all-day event?" I asked.

"First of all, I'm not driving, you are. Secondly, I'll take my pillow and sit in the back seat. I'm moving forward in my life."

Vivid images flashed before my eyes of Jersey and her idiot older sister hitting me and a neighbor with switches on the walk from school to home. "Trade Jersey for Nettie?"

Rosa Leigh placed her plate in the dishwasher and glared at me. "Nettie is taking a car load of women herself."

"I'll go with her. I'll call her and have one of her riders switch with me."

"Stop it," Rosa Leigh snapped. "You and Jersey are adults, and this is forty some years later. You need to forgive and forget. She's changed. We are to pick her up in an hour and a half. I advise you to dress."

When we arrived at Jersey's later, the house didn't surprise me. She came from money. The executive style, two-story home nestled the hillside at the end of a long driveway. She was outside, her overnight bag in hand. Her once black, kinky hair was now snow white, and she used a four-prong cane. Her wrinkled face looked like a prune.

Janene hopped out to help her load her suitcase. I'm glad she did because I wasn't doing it. I was driving today, and if she gave me any of her former attitude, I'd leave her on the side of the road.

Rosa Leigh glanced to her left and said, "Jersey, I'm happy you could go today." She nodded my way.

Jersey snorted. "You should've put me with Nettie where I would be safe."

I unsnapped my seat belt and swiveled around, "When I discovered you were in this car, *I* wanted to ride with Nettie."

She tut-tutted.

I re-buckled myself and drove away so fast her head hit the seat. I kicked myself mentally for allowing the sight of her and her wicked mouth to torment me.

"We have plenty of time. The play isn't until 2:45," Rosa Leigh said, obviously trying to break the tension. She looked at her watch. "It's 10:00 now, and if all goes as planned, we can stop for lunch, potty breaks, check into our rooms and still have time to relax a few minutes."

Janene began her endless questions about the area, and my anger dissipated...slowly. We made good time and were almost to Portsmouth, Ohio, when Jersey announced she needed to use the "lady's washroom."

"Cross your legs and hold it," I said. "You know there are no rest areas until we are on the other side of Portsmouth."

Jersey leaned forward. "You've heard of restaurants. With your maniac driving, I could also use a cup of coffee or tea."

I glanced at Rosa Leigh. "If she starts with her annoying demands, I'll wring her neck like a chicken."

Rosa Leigh smiled, and looked at Jersey. "We'll stop at the rest area. We'll be there . . ." she paused to look at her watch, ". . . in about twenty minutes or so."

Jersey harrumphed. "You better hope I don't soil myself."

An entertaining image filled my mind.

"We'll let you out if you have an emergency. You can go in the bushes or beside the road." I visualized that sight and giggled. "It would be a car stopper, I'm sure."

I glanced in the rearview mirror, and she lifted her royal chin, letting us know the act was beneath her.

Ten minutes later we were crossing the bridge over the Ohio River.

We stopped for two lights going through the city, and soon I was driving into a parking space at the rest area. Jersey opened her door and scuttled to the bathroom. Janene and Rosa Leigh remained in the car. I slipped out. My philosophy on the open road was to use the bathroom every opportunity. One never knew when she'd be stalled in traffic for hours.

As I used the toilet, Jersey was in the handicap stall, using not so royal language. I opened the door and walked to the sink to wash my hands. Her highness slammed her stall door against the wall. She waddled out, holding her pants around her thighs. Liquid streamed to the floor. And a body of water was chasing her out of the stall.

I grabbed my face with both hands. "What on earth?!"

Jersey wobbled around and looked inside where she'd been. Her white flabby butt glared at me. "The automatic toilet attacked me!"

"Your clothes are soaked!"

She glowered at me and pointed to the toilet. "I sat down, began to tinkle, and I felt this ice-cold water on my derriere. Then, it hit the floor and splashed my legs and shoes. The darn the thing flushed before I was done. Startled, I jumped up, and I was still urinating." She had her hands on her knees, still in a half-bend. "I waded through sewer water to the tissue paper. In the process, I knocked my cane down, and I can't pick it up."

She straightened, yanked and tugged at her dripping capris and yelled, "Wipe the smile off your face and go get my overnight bag and bring it to me!"

My neck burned, my face heated up and my jaw cracked. But, I bowed, and said, "Yes, my Queen." I turned and marched to the car.

When I opened the door, Janene asked, "Where's Jersey?"

Hoping my smile wouldn't give me away, I said, "She'll be here soon."

Janene and Rosa Leigh continued chatting.

In a few minutes, Jersey tramped toward the car, her cane hitting the sidewalk so hard, the clink echoed through the entire rest area. She yanked open the door and scowled at me. "Thank you, Ives...for nothing! I humiliated myself. . ." she waved her hand through the air and continued, "...in front of all these people. I hope you're happy now."

As I remembered the hundreds of times that she rubbed my nose in the dirt, squirted mustard or ketchup in my hair and yelled mean things in front of the class, I asked over my shoulders. "How does it feel?"

She ranted on, "The toilet decided to flush all by itself. It was clogged. Thank goodness, it was clean water and didn't smell like a sewer." She struggled into the car. "Look at all the people staring. They think I wet myself."

I felt a twinge of guilt as I drove back onto Route 23. I listened as the others talked. When we reached the next rest area, forty-five miles north, Jersey asked to stop again. We spent a half hour there while she cleaned herself up and changed into dry clothing.

My body language must have been warning enough for Janene and Rosa Leigh. Neither asked questions. When Jersey returned, we continued our trip.

I glanced in the mirror occasionally. Jersey was gazing out the window, her shoulders sagging. She didn't appear as haughty as before, but I knew she'd be back to her queenie way soon.

Rosa Leigh recalculated our schedule and said, "We won't have time to check into the room. If we make our next bathroom break at a restaurant, though, we will make the play on time."

Later at the theater, I followed Rosa Leigh through the aisle to our designated seats. She whispered over her shoulder, "I'm so glad the staples aren't bothering me, the drain tubes aren't a problem, and I feel well enough to be here. After the first chemo, my activities will be curtailed."

She motioned me to a row of seats half-filled with members of her reading group. I sidestepped to the first empty seat, almost at the end of the row, and waited for her, but she remained at the end of the aisle. She gave me an absent-minded wave and said, "I need to be here to direct late stragglers."

The lights dimmed, voices softened, and music blared. I looked at the person in the seat next to mine. I didn't want to sit here, but the other seats were now filled. As I sat down next to Ms. Overstreet, she leaned over and whispered, "I won't tell Danita."

I told her I'd change seats during intermission, but she shook her head and whispered, "I have a secret to tell you during the break."

I bounced my right leg. The last thing I needed was for Danita to press charges for me violating the five hundred-foot restraining order. I squirmed, crossed and uncrossed my ankles and picked at my nails until intermission.

As soon as the curtains closed, I stood to make my escape. Ms. Overstreet grabbed my hand. "Will you help me to the lady's room?"

A knot hardened in my chest. "If we are seen together, and we will be, someone will tell your daughter. I promised my friend and the Sheriff I wouldn't violate the order. Who did you ride with? She'll take you."

"I want it to be you."

As the two of us entered the restroom, Rosa Leigh stared at me. I shrugged. She took the older lady's arm. "Let me help you. Ives needs to use the facilities, and I'm free."

Ms. Overstreet wrestled her arm lose. "No thank you, dear." She pushed past Rosa Leigh, and her cane click-clacked all the way to the handicap stall.

By the time the two of us had done our business, everyone was gone. She propped her cane against the counter and turned on the water. "I have the skull. My nephews found it when they followed a trail from our woods up the mountain. They thought someone might be making moonshine on our property, or worse, bringing drugs into the county. They brought it to me. They thought it might belong to my brother. He went up the mountain to tend a still years ago and was never seen again. If it's him, I couldn't rest knowing the rest of him is up there, somewhere. And, I wanted a burial, if it was him."

She tore off a paper towel and dried her hands.

"After I learned you were up there snooping, I asked them to take it to my son's friend in Columbus. He studies bones, the friend, I mean. He told me what to send him besides the skull. I sent a tattered cap I couldn't bring myself to get rid of." She tossed the paper towel into the trash. "Said he'd run tests because my son was his best friend. The doc said he could get in big trouble if he didn't let the law here in the county know." She retrieved her cane, took my arm and tugged at me. "Tell the Sheriff to call. I'll give him the bone man's phone number. That'll give me time to tell my daughter about the skull."

I scratched my head.

Can I trust her?

"Thank you, I think."

She opened the door. "You can trust me. Sometimes, when I first wake up, I forget where I am. It's them dang drugs the doctor gives me. In no time, though, I remember things. Reckon I do act downright goofy at times, but I ain't."

After the show, when the lights came on, Rosa Leigh waved for her group to gather around her. "For those of you who chose not to eat dinner, Ives, Janene and I packed cheese, crackers and some cookies. We'll leave the door open a little. Come by to refresh yourself and chat about the show."

Nettie raised her hand. "I brought wine."

The ladies clapped.

She held up her hand and said, "If you don't mind drinking out of plastic glasses."

Red chimed in, "I'll drink out of the bottle if I have to."

We laughed and walked to the cars, chatting. I drove to our hotel. The valet took our luggage to the room while we checked in. To say I was surprised about the large size of our suite and the extra amenities in our room would be a lie. Rosa Leigh reserved what she liked, and she never went for anything less than the best available. And since she was paying, we didn't complain.

By the time the three of us were in our night clothes, the others filtered in. The seating arrangement wasn't great for that many extra people. There was a recliner and two king size beds, so most didn't stay long.

Nettie and Maggie stretched out on the beds with us. The five of us were leaning against the headboards discussing the play when what sounded like heavy feet thudded past our room.

A deep, very base voice shouted, "Police! Hands in the air."

The five of us froze. A woman screamed and mumbled something, and the male voice boomed again, "Last time. Stand up and put your hands in the air."

A different female voice said, "There's no need to put handcuffs on her. She's too old to out-run us."

The door down the hall closed, and the hall was quiet. I looked at Rosa Leigh. Her mouth was open, and her eyes were huge. The others had the same shocked expressions. I grabbed my phone off the bedside table and punch 9-1-1. I explained what happened and told them the location. A man on the other end told me a car was on the way and to stay inside our room. I disconnected the call.

Nettie slid out of bed, tiptoed to the door and closed it. "Do you suppose it's a drug dealer? Or a murderer?" She grabbed her head with both hands and paced. "Doesn't matter. I'm not leaving until they're gone."

Maggie said, "Me either." She snatched up a wine bottle and guzzled, until Janene pried it from her hands. Nettie stuffed a cheese square and a cracker into her mouth.

A door opened at the end of the hall, and the noise level in that direction rose. We cocked our best ears towards the door.

"You better be telling the truth," the deep voice said, growing louder.

And then...BOOM! BOOM! BOOM!

The knock rattled our door. "Police."

I climbed out of the bed and inched toward the door.

Another BOOM jarred the other ladies off the bed.

Rosa Leigh grabbed her gun out of her bag.

The voice from outside the door yelled again. "Police! Open up!"

I peeked through the hole, saw a badge against the glass and opened the door, shooting my hands into the air.

I stared at the woman standing between the two uniformed officers. "What did you do, Jersey?"

She burst into tears and blubbered indistinguishable words.

A handsome, brown-skinned male said, "She was playing Cinderella and sleeping in the bear's bed." He chuckled at his joke.

I looked from Jersey to him. "I thought Cinderella was the one whose coach turned into a pumpkin"

The female officer stuck her palm in my face and asked, "Do you know this lady?"

I nodded.

Unlocking the cuffs, the guy said, "She tells this cock-a-mammie story about being directionally challenged and how she is to meet you women for snacks. Instead, she goes to the wrong room and finds it empty. She helps herself to the owner's food and decides to rest while she waits for all of you to arrive. The occupant was searching for the ice machine and returned to find her sleeping in his bed." He looked at Jersey. "Did I tell all the significant details?"

She nodded, reached inside her bra, pulled out a lace-trimmed handkerchief and blew.

He rolled his eyes and said, "Is this looney tunes telling the truth?"

"Yes," I said. "She was supposed to come here for snacks."

He looked at his partner. "We can't charge her with breaking and entering, because the simpleton left the door standing ajar while he goes down the hall to get ice. I don't want the paperwork, anyway." He walked away. The lady cop trailed.

Jersey turned and hobbled in the correct direction to her room.

Deep inside, my altruistic trait rose. I tried so hard to stuff it down, but as the frail soul who had taunted me as a child and then today as well used the card to unlock her door, I decided I had to do something.

When I touched her shoulder, she jerked away, keeping her head down. "Did you come to gloat and poke fun at the ignorant woman?"

Angry with myself for choosing this moment to feel a tug of my conscience, I drew a stuttering breath and said, "No. I came to apologize for not returning with your clothes at the rest area."

She bit her lower lip. "You were mean."

The light turned green, and she entered her room. "But I guess you owe me a lot more."

Tossing the key card on the desk, she motioned me in. "I don't expect you to forgive me for all the rotten things I did to you back then, but I am sorry. There aren't many days I don't think about how evil I was." She threw up her hands. "No excuse. And today, I have nightmares of all you mistreated people ganging up on me. Like I said, I can't undo anything. But I'm trying to do better."

She walked to the sink and turned on the water. In the mirror, her eyes flicked up and focused on me. "Didn't have no choice. My hatred was eating me up. The psychiatrist said I needed to let the past go. I did."

Standing in the doorway, I wrapped my fingers around the knob. "Do you think you and I could ever be friends?"

Her breath hitched in her chest. "It will take a lot of work."

"We can start by being civil to each other when we're together."

Jersey turned to me. "Okay."

I closed the door behind me and walked to my room. As I strolled back, the world lifted off my shoulders. This trip had been good for all of us.

And I couldn't wait to tell Blake the news about the skull.

Chapter 28

When we arrived home the next morning, Blake's cruiser was in Rosa Leigh's driveway. As Rosa Leigh, Janene and I scrambled out of the car and retrieved our luggage from the trunk, he came around the corner of the house and hastened to help us.

"Good morning, Lovely Ladies. Simon is fed and watered. Did you all have a good time?" He asked.

I handed him Rosa Leigh's makeup and jewelry bag. It weighed a ton. The other two ladies ignored us and clamored on to each other about the show we'd seen.

"Did you enjoy your trip?" He asked.

I nodded. "The show was the only relaxing thing, though."

He followed to the house, through the kitchen, across the dining room and down the hall to Rosa Leigh's room.

"You're too quiet. Did the drive tire you?"

I punched his shoulder. "Do you think I'm old and can't handle that? No! I'm not tired from the trip. There were lots of crazy and nerve-wracking things going on."

"Don't keep me in suspense then. Spill," he said and stepped closer, concern written all over his handsome face.

I pushed him into Rosa Leigh's room and snickered. "Put her bags on the bed. You'll need more time than you have today for me to tell you about our weekend."

"I'll pick you up for dinner this evening, and you can tell me about it."

We placed the luggage in the respective rooms all of it belonged in, and he met me in the hall. I walked him to the kitchen door, and when I opened it, Simon was looking up at me, his tail wagging. But when I noticed the prize he dropped on the deck, the air gushed from my lungs.

A skull!

He barked.

Blake picked it up. "Someone's shot it, and then couldn't find it. Most men don't hunt for sport in these parts. They don't waste meat."

"It's an eight-point buck. Where's the lower jaw?" I asked, finally finding my voice.

Blake held the skull to his chest and fingered the lower bones. "Looks like other animals found it and ate the meat. The rest is up there on the mountain somewhere." He laid it on the swing and patted Simon on the head. "Good job, buddy."

Simon wagged his tail.

Puzzled, I asked, "Did you let him go hunting?"

"He wasn't out of my sight until I saw the car in the drive and let him outside. I'd say he had this stashed somewhere nearby. Dogs often hide or bury their hunt."

I stroked Simon's fur. "You stinker. Why didn't you find the skull you and I searched for?"

Blake went around the dog, and Simon and I followed him to his cruiser. The static of his radio echoed through the air as we neared the car. He jogged ahead and answered the call. "What's up, Rick?"

There's a loud click and more static. The person on the other end, evidently named Rick, spoke, "Your informant says now would be a good time to check out the cave for illegal activity. The men are working days at a job south of Lexington and won't return until dark."

Blake pushed the button and responded, "Thanks. I'm at the Adams' place now. I'll check it out." He disconnected, walked to the back of his cruiser, took a pair of hiking boots from the trunk and leaned against the car to change into them.

I ran to the house, my voice trailing behind me, "I'm coming with you!"

"This is police work, not a nature hike. You will not!" Blake yelled out.

Ten minutes later, I scurried out the back door and made my way to where I'd left him. But he was gone.

I raced behind the house, looked toward the mountain, but there was no sign of him. As I walked toward the trees, I mumbled, "I know where the cave is, Sheriff. I don't need you."

Simon followed me. I tried to chase him back, but he was as stubborn as I was. He waited for me to walk ahead a distance, as if to make sure we were really doing this, and then came up running up right next to me.

As I parted the brush and stepped into the thicket, he thrashed through it. He looked at me and wagged his tail. "Come on." I waved for him. "Maybe your size will scare the criminals. Or…maybe you'll drown them in your slobbers while licking them."

I couldn't believe how fast Blake was hiking. I stopped long enough to drink water and give a little to Simon and kept trekking. I hoped to catch up with him. I certainly didn't want to wander into the cavern alone.

As our trips before, the gnarled undergrowth grabbed at my feet and legs, each step feeling as if I were walking on moist sponges. Testing the area with my feet so I didn't slip or fall into a ravine slowed me way down, but since I was carrying only the necessities – flashlight, food and water, the lighter load wasn't tiring me as much.

I recognized my landmarks and realized Blake was also using the trail Simon and I had made. With that discovery, it didn't seem as frightening as the two of us snuck beneath the shadows of the trees. The squeal of a hawk and the skittering of a rabbit crossing in front didn't even startle us as it usually did. We were on a mission to make sure Blake wasn't alone at that cave.

When I reached the familiar steep, rocky path near the cave, a brisk wind kicked up debris and swirled it through the air. I stumbled on, blinking silt from my eyes and jumped a foot when Blake spoke up.

"It's a good thing for you two those men are miles away. Your tramping sounds reached halfway up the incline."

I trudged on. "Thanks for waiting."

He walked ahead of us through the mouth of the cave. "One of these days, you're going to wish you'd listened to people when they warn you."

To calm his anger, I changed the topic. "It's a wonder the teenagers aren't using this as their hangout."

The flashlight beam danced over the ceiling. It was covered with bats. When I jiggled the beam back and forth, one screeched and fluttered. Fascinated, I waved the light up and down and around the hundreds roosting on the ceiling. Suddenly, one of creatures torpedoed me, darting and squealing. I covered my head with my arms. Pain shot up to my shoulder. Blake grabbed my arm and pulled me through the first opening we came to. None too soon, either. One struck the glass on my flashlight as we ducked into the tunnel.

Blake walked fast, and I jogged to keep up. He chattered on as if I hadn't been nearly killed by a bat. "I doubt any of the local teens know where this cave is. They claimed a few on some of the ridges. The walls are peppered with their names, dates and drawings."

I figured Blake was looking for a moonshine still, or the makings of a meth lab or storage units for illegal substances. "What's so wrong with the men making their own moonshine? My dad had a still and sold it. It put food on our table. You and a few of Rosa Leigh's boyfriends stole a few quarts, as I recall. You loved his corn liquor."

He whistled. "It was the best around, colorless and tasteless White Lightning."

I scoffed. "It tasted like pure alcohol and burned all the way down."

"I don't expect to find a still in here. Most are hidden way up under a cliff, near a stream and are usually protected by impenetrable thickets. I'm searching for the product those men are storing. You said they're making trips in with bags over their shoulders, and someone else takes them out."

"Maybe they have a meth lab in here."

He glanced over his shoulder. "No, they use their kitchens for the cooking."

Soon, we came to a little stream trickling over a ledge, carrying limestone sediment with it. A small waterfall had formed. We stood in awe and enjoyed its beauty, and then journeyed on.

Blake marked the wall with a permanent marker from time to time as we wound this way and the other into the scary depths of the cave. In one place, we found a spacious cavern with stalactites the size of his leg, and when the light slithered across, it glimmered. There were several openings, and I followed him through one.

After a while, we found a spring. Its basin was crusted with glittering crystals that looked like frost. We kneeled, cupped our hands and drank the cold, clear water.

Once we quenched our thirst, we started through a corridor and walked in silence. I glanced at each new opening to see if there was anything familiar about it, but I didn't recognize anything. I guess I'd been scared sillier than I thought when those men had pushed and prodded me through.

"Do you know where we are?" I asked, after we'd walked through several more channels.

He took off his cap and scratched his head. "No, but I marked the walls behind. So, relax."

I followed him through more narrow passageways into other large caverns, but there was no sign of human activity. Finally, Blake said, "We might as well go back to the entryway and try another tunnel."

I trailed behind him and Simon as we passed the glittering waterfall, the room with the leg-size stalactites, and I held my breath as we passed beneath the bats again. This time, I kept my light pointed at the ground. We passed without disturbing them and walked a short distance to the entryway.

"Let's go outside for fresh air before we search through another passage," Blake said.

He stepped into the daylight and stopped.

I pushed my way around him and Simon and found myself staring into the barrel of a sawed-off shotgun.

Blake was looking into the barrel of a .22 rifle.

I eased closer to him and whispered, "They weren't working. Or they got off early." Either way, we were in big trouble.

Both faces were covered with bandanas. One was a head taller than the other, and since they were also wearing caps, I couldn't see their hair. I couldn't tell if it was the same two who'd abducted me.

The tall one stepped forward.

Simon growled and bared his teeth.

"Control the dog, or I'll shoot it."

I pushed Simon's backside down and smoothed his fur, calming him. "It's okay."

"Turn around and fall to your knees."

Blake kneeled and told me to follow suit.

I did.

The stones behind us crunched.

There was a dull thump, and he fell over onto his side.

Simon barked and lunged at the tall guy.

Another dull sound echoed through the air, Simon yelped and snuggled next to me.

I squeezed my eyes tight, waiting.

Slate rocks clunked together as the attackers strolled a few feet away.

One of the men said, "Why'd you hit him? You might've hurt him bad or killed him."

The taller one answered, "I didn't. This is not my first time to knock someone out. We need time to be long gone when he wakes."

The first one warned, "You're not hurting her. She reminds me of my grandmother."

Thank God. I'll keep my big mouth shut this time and let him call me any name he chooses.

They walked further away where only snatches of their conversation filtered through the air. The tall one wanted to take us deep into the cave. The other argued, "Guy . . . heavy."

The shorter one, the guy who appeared to be the boss, crunched back to where we were, riffled through Blake's pocket and took out his cell phone. Then, he dug through my bag. He was so close I smelled his stale cigarette smoke.

The stones were digging deeper into my knees, but I didn't dare squirm. Or breathe. And I was so worried about Blake I was beyond panic.

The guy dropped my pack on the ground near me, lifted the tail of my t-shirt at the back and took my phone out of my back pocket.

I remained on my aching knees until their footsteps faded and then crawled to Blake. He had a lump the size of a goose egg on the back of his head, but the skin wasn't torn. I jerked my arm away when something wet touched it. It was Simon. I buried my face in his fur and sobbed.

When I stopped crying, I searched Blake's pocket and found his marker and his notebook and scribbled a note to Rosa Leigh.

Blake's injured. Send someone with stretcher.

I searched through his other pockets to find something to attach the note to Simon, but I couldn't find anything. Rummaging through my bag, fear knotted in my stomach. I couldn't find a useful tool.

I tapped my head. *Think! Think!* And finally, my brain cells fired.

Unlacing the string from one of Blake's hiking boots, I used the plastic tip on the ends to punch a hole through the paper, working one end through and around Simon's collar, and tied them.

"Find help, Boy," I said and waved him down the mountain.

He sprung into action and disappeared over the hill.

I turned to Blake and said, "Nothing for us to do now but wait." When he didn't answer, fear slithered over me like a blanket of doom, and I prayed, "God, please send help."

Chapter 29

Since I don't wear a watch and the heavy, overhead foliage blocked the sun, I didn't know how long Simon had been gone. It didn't' matter anyway, except to tell me how long Blake had been unconscious. It seemed like hours.

I gently shook him again, and he groaned.

"Hey you. Wake up. We need to get off this mountain before dark."

One eye fluttered, and he moaned more. I splashed water from the bottle in my pack onto his face. He swiped it off and opened his eyes.

"What happened?"

"One of the guys hit you over the head with his gun. Can you sit up?"

He struggled to a sitting position and rubbed the goose egg on his head. Wincing, he pushed himself up and staggered. "Got any more water?"

I handed him the half-empty container, and he drank the rest. He scanned the ground above the cave. "Will you bring me one of those large sticks lying up there? It will help me keep my balance."

I scaled the knoll, picked up the pole and walked back down the incline. He took the aide and hobbled down the trail.

"Where's your backpack?" I asked. "You might have supplies we need before we reach the bottom."

He turned and smiled sheepishly. "I'm the big brave cop. I came without one, if you recall." He limped on.

"If you're hungry, I have packs of peanut butter and cheese crackers and another bottle of water we can share. I packed light, too."

"I'm okay for now. Thank you."

The air warmed as we descended. It was filled with scents of dried leaves and dead plantlife. Katydids were chirping, grasshoppers were jumping on twigs as we passed, and a squirrel scurried up a tree with half a nut exposed in its mouth. Lost in my memories of the days I'd roamed these hillsides, I was jarred when I slammed into Blake's back.

He whispered, "Don't twitch a muscle."

"What is it?"

"Listen."

There was a rattling sound in the weeds. And it was near. I couldn't tell the direction it was coming from. The two of us stood like statues. All at once, the grass to our right rustled. A rabbit darted out. The rattle went faster, and zoom, the snake stretched no more than a foot in front of Blake and clamped its fangs into the rabbit.

"Go," Blake said.

I ran as fast as my jelly legs would carry me, and he hurried behind.

After we'd gotten far enough away, he said, "You can slow down now."

I stopped, and gulping deep breaths, I asked, "Why didn't you kill it?"

He took a deep breath to match mine. "Acting the big brave cop again." He threw up his hands and chuckled. "Until the snake struck, I didn't know where it was, but I knew it was close. If you can't run, standing still is the best defense. Snakes don't attack unless they're frightened. The rattle was the warning to keep away. You remember this, correct? We were taught as toddlers to protect ourselves from them."

I wiped my beaded brow with my sleeve. "Forty years has passed, and my memory of what to do is gone. I'm glad you were here and knew."

He tramped down the mountain.

I paid much closer attention to the path the rest of the trip. We were over halfway down the mountain, when we heard voices. Blake motioned me to a thicket at the side of the trail. We squatted and waited.

I recognized a familiar voice and stood up.

"What are you doing here, Nettie Stamper?" I scolded, even though I was so happy to see her.

She came into view, followed by a young officer who looked to be mid-twenties, slim and muscular. I thought it might be the Rick I'd heard on Blake's radio.

"She insisted on carrying one end of the stretcher. The EMTs will be awhile, so I decided to bring ours," the officer said, looking at Blake for approval.

Blake slapped the officer on the back. "Smart choice, Rick. You came prepared, but I can make it the rest of the way."

Blake motioned us forward.

"I guess the informant was wrong about the guys working out of town today," Rick said over his shoulder. "Or this might not be the same two men."

I spoke up. "They didn't intend to kill us. I overheard them talking, and I think they were as surprised as we were. They simply wanted to leave."

We hiked in silence awhile, until Rick asked, "Did you find any sign of a still or drugs?"

Blake sighed. "No. There are so many caverns and channels in there. It will take a team to explore all of them. When we're back at the office, Rick, you contact the locals who are not working tomorrow, and we'll go up and search the whole cave."

While the two men discussed business, I asked Nettie, "How did you know Blake and I needed help?"

She quipped in an angry tone. "Like I always do when it concerns you."

"Did you have one of your visions?" As soon as I asked, I was sorry I did. She didn't like for anyone else to talk about her "second sight thingy."

"It was a feeling that something was wrong."

I prodded her, dying to know more about her skills. "You saw me in trouble?"

Nettie stopped, crossed her arms across her chest and said, "It's more of a premonition. Like I said, more of a feeling. I don't *see* you."

Rick piped up, "Have you got a premonition on who is using the cave, or what they might be storing and exchanging up there?"

The back of Nettie's neck reddened.

I felt terrible that I'd mentioned her gift or talent or magical skill or whatever you called what happens to her. But I was glad it was her and not me. "Don't be snide,

Deputy. Her powers are difficult for people to understand sometimes, but they are real."

Nettie cleared her throat. "Most of my premonitions are about people I have a close relationship with."

I tugged her blouse and whispered, "Sorry I mentioned this."

Rick said, "I believe you, Ms. Nettie. My grandmother was like you. She scared the devil out of me more than once when I was a kid, but she was always right."

"I'm thinking that's enough chatter for now," Blake said. "Silence allows us to hear the rattle of a snake, right, Ives?"

The talking ceased for the rest of the trip.

When we stepped into the sunshine, Janene rose from the lounge chair on the deck and ran across the five acres towards us. Simon raced to meet us, too. When we finally reached each other, she said, "We told the emergency squad to stop here so we could point them to the trail into the woods. It's great to—"

Wailing sirens drowned out her voice as EMT trucks squealed to a stop in front of Rosa Leigh's, leaving a trail of dust. Men and women burst out of the vehicles and ran towards us. As we reached the deck, an EMT guided Blake to the chair and began to examine him.

I waved the other EMT away and told her I was okay. As I watched Blake being loaded into the ambulance, my mind drifted back up the mountain.

I know something illegal is going on in the cave, and I'm going to find out who they are and what crime they're committing.

Chapter 30

A lot happened the rest of the afternoon. The EMTs took Blake to the hospital to check out his head injury. Rick returned to the office to make calls for volunteers to search the cave the next day. Rosa Leigh and Janene listened intently as I told all the minute details of the ordeal.

Janene took notes and as soon as I finished, she excused herself. She wasn't fooling me.

She was going right to her desk to pen the next chapter, which was going to be all about Blake's and my excursion on the mountain.

Rosa Leigh took a nap and by the time she woke up, Blake had been released from the hospital and made plans with me for dinner.

After my shower, I was putting on my earrings for our date when the doorbell chimed. I opened it to find Ms. Overstreet on the stoop. My breath caught in my throat, and I clutched my chest. "I'll call Rosa Leigh."

"No, I came to talk to you. May I come in?"

"Of course."

She entered and looked back to the drive. Someone in a beat-up red truck waved.

"They can come in, too," I said.

"He's my nephew, Shine's son. His dad, my brother, went to prison for making and selling moonshine, and is in a nursing home now. I'm the only family him and his brother have here, and we're close. They run me places I need to go and wait for me, like they did their mom. He's a good boy."

I motioned for her to sit in a chair in the living room.

Using her cane, she hobbled across the room to it and had a seat.

"May I bring you something to drink?"

She shook her head. "This is not a social call, though I hope we have some in the future. I enjoy your company." She bent and took something wrapped in a bath towel out of a cloth bag and handed it to me. "I believe you are searching for this. I need to tell you what I know about it."

Laying the object in my lap, I unwrapped it.

Blood rushed to my brain so fast it sounded like a train roaring through my ears. My heart pounded like a jackhammer against my chest.

"You got it back?!"

"I did," she said and took a tissue from beneath her watch band, blotted her forehead and continued, "I want to tell the truth about my missing brother. He robbed a bank with two other men who were killed. Wounded, my brother got away and made it to the mountain. Dogs tracked him to the foothills, but the other Sheriff told us he got away. We didn't believe that no-account law man because our brother would've contacted his wife or one of us."

She wiped the corners of her eyes with the tissue and went on, "All these years, we've searched for his bones, but never found a sign until my nephews found the skull on top of a cave when they searched for some trespassers. It belongs to my brother."

She took a folder out of the bag and handed it to me. "There's a copy of the report my friend sent. You can give the skull and the report to Sheriff Blake."

She stood.

I put the skull on the end table and followed her to the door.

"Danita knows everything now. I'm sorry she had you arrested. At the time, I couldn't tell her what I was doing. I hadn't sent the skull to Columbus yet. Now that this is behind us, you can come for coffee. We always have pie or cake around, too." She smiled and the corners of her eyes crinkled.

I touched her bony arm. "I was searching for the skull one of the days two men were there. Why would your nephews wear bandanas over their faces?"

"They had no need to do that," she said and stared at me in stunned surprise. "Like I said, my nephews were looking for trespassers and found the skull. They told me they followed the trail off the mountain without seeing anyone."

"Your nephews were probably the ones thrashing through the brush who scared me away one time I returned for the skull. Perhaps not the men in the bandanas then. Again, thank you."

As she limped to the truck, her nephew rushed to help her up into the cab. They both waved goodbye.

Won't Rosa Leigh be surprised. I'll show it to her later.

As I closed the closet door where I stashed the treasure, the bell chimed.

The sight of Blake made my stomach quiver. I intended to tell him about the skull, but I didn't want to spoil the moment. *A few more hours are not going to make a difference.*

He smiled and kissed my cheek. "Wow! Look at you. You're beautiful. Blue makes your white hair even more striking."

"You're still such a smooth talker," I said, basking in his sweet words.

"We're having dinner at a restaurant about an hour away."

"Why not Nettie's?"

"I want you all to myself tonight," he said and winked. "At her place, she'll buzz around like a bee, and this restaurant's a little more upscale."

On the way, we talked about family and friends.

All at once, he snapped his fingers. "Rick and some men staked out the cave. They caught three men and, according to Rick, two of the men were transporting supplies over the mountain to another guy who makes meth. Supposedly, my men and I know the roads, the users and the pushers too well and forced the new men to find other routes."

I told him then about Ms. Overstreet bringing the skull and recapped the story of how her nephews found it by following the trail of trespassers. He agreed with me that the proper thing to do was to let Ms. Overstreet have it back since it was her brother's...once the report was verified and the anthropologist said he was officially releasing the bones, that is.

Blake told me next about a tourist discovering a body on Dry Ridge Mountain, near where the teenager's car was abandoned. The boy's wallet with his driver's license was found lying among the remains along with a class ring engraved with his name still on the finger bone.

Blake stared into space and said, "Finding a body and telling the next of kin is a part of my job I'll never get used to."

Cars and scenery flitted by the window in a blur, and before I knew it, Blake pulled into a parking lot. It was already dusk, and I wondered where the time had gone.

The building looked like a castle. It was surrounded by acres and acres of farmland with crops in the fields. One plot was dotted orange with pumpkins. Alfalfa spread to the horizon. Corn, taller than Blake's five-foot nine frame and ready to pick, bordered fields of ripe soybeans on the other side of the four-lane highway.

Inside, a pretty hostess in a white blouse and black dress pants greeted and led us to a secluded table. A candle flickered in a crystal bowl in the center, and a white rayon tablecloth covered the table. Soft piano music played in the background.

As soon as we were seated, a waiter appeared, took my napkin from the plate and placed it on my lap. Drinks were ordered – water for each of us. Neither of us were ever drinkers. The waiter hustled away.

Blake looked at me. "I've missed you. And I'm glad you're here."

"Me, too," I answered him.

Silence lingered between us. And I wasn't accustomed to quiet. Most of my friends talk over each other. With Blake, we've always had times when neither of us spoke. Enjoying the moment, I gazed into his intense blue eyes that were focused on me.

"Are you seeing anyone in Florida?"

"No. Do you have a steady?"

He squirmed in the seat. "Did Rosa Leigh tell you about all the women?"

"She mentioned it our first evening at Nettie's. She said you take a different woman to dinner every night," I said, most interested in his response.

He bristled. "She did?! She's in for an earful then."

He leaned forward and placed his forearms on the table. "The only women I've taken to dinner since my wife's death have been for business meetings."

I coughed. "Uh huh. And why did you have the blond out three or four times?"

"I was interviewing her for a position in the Sheriff's Office. She was interested in the Dispatcher's opening."

I placed my elbows on the table and leaned in. "And it took three or four dinners to determine if she was qualified?"

A sly smile spread across his face. "Am I detecting jealousy?"

My heart fluttered. He was, but I wasn't about to admit it. "Of course not. But the job doesn't appear to be so complex to me that it would require that many meetings about it."

"To be truthful, I'm called out a lot, even during meetings. We only have four men, and my office covers the entire county, and finding the right dispatcher will relieve me of having to answer the calls myself."

The waiter placed a large bowl of salad on the table and asked if we would like cheese. We indicated we did, and he shredded it over the greens.

When he left, Blake asked, "How is Rosa Leigh?" He forked salad into his mouth.

"The oncologist says she's doing great. She's a fighter and has a positive attitude about the whole thing. There haven't been any melt downs since the diagnosis."

He lifted his glass, and we toasted her.

"Tell me about Janene's novel," he said. "How's she coming on it?"

"Your guess is as good as mine. She hasn't said. But it's about a woman who is close to solving a murder, but the killer is determined to keep their identity a secret."

"Sounds like a page turner."

"She says she's using our adventures upon the mountain in the book. I can't wait until its done, and she lets me read it."

The waiter appeared with our dinners. He placed a steaming hot plate of chicken scampi in front of me and a steak and baked potato for Blake. After he left, we continued to talk. Our conversation covered religion, our own mates and our families.

While we waited for coffee and chocolate mousse, he asked, "Will you stay to help Rosa Leigh since you've solved the case of the skull? Or will you return with Janene to continue your private eye business?"

"When Janene knows about the skull, she'll want to return to Florida. She only came here to babysit me and keep me out of trouble while I solved the case." I laughed at the absurdity of her intentions. "The Skyway Bridge is open now, and air flight is returning slowly. I haven't checked in a day or two to see if we can fly into St. Petersburg, Tampa or Sarasota."

"Do you need to return? I think Rosa Leigh needs you now."

Is there any chance you need me?

"My home remained standing. I lost a carport, but Jake called someone to replace it." I placed my hands in my lap, making room for the waiter to serve the mousse.

"Is Jake the maintenance man?"

When I told him that Jake is a friend who lives behind me, he put his fork on his plate and took a drink of coffee.

The whole time his intense blue eyes were locked on mine. "Are you in a relationship with him?"

I laughed until tears streamed down my cheeks.

He shrugged and waited for me to regain my composure.

"Our relationship might be one step deeper than you and your business dates," I said and winked, taking a tissue from my purse and dabbing at my eyes. "I take him desserts sometimes, and I worked with him on one of my PI cases."

I thought about it some more and swiped my hands as I were erasing a dry erase board. "He retired recently from the police department. When we needed someone on the inside to gain pertinent information on a case, I asked him to be our eyes and ears. In fact, Janene and the other partners asked him to help in the future. He agreed." I leaned in closer to Blake. "Do I detect a bit of jealousy?"

He grinned. "Could this Jake take care of the carport and check the inside of your home for leaks?"

I put my napkin on the table and pushed away my dessert dish. "I gave him the extra key."

Blake cocked a brow.

"He's one of the few men in the complex who putters with remodeling in his spare time, and he knows about electricity and plumbing. Not knowing how long it would take to solve the skull case, I thought if something went wrong, he could fix it without my rushing back," I said, so tickled that Blake was concerned.

Blake's body relaxed. "Good answer."

After he paid the bill using one of those cool table scanners, he rose from his seat. "Ready?"

He took hold of my chair and pulled it out.

The ride home was more small talk, and when we arrived, he walked me to the door. "I enjoyed this evening. Will you join me again tomorrow night?"

"I'd love to." I lifted my head, waiting for him to kiss me.

And I waited...

Being only five-foot-four to his five-foot nine, my neck was in such a crook, my muscles spasmed.

But he doesn't kiss me.

I rummaged in my purse for the keys and unlocked the door. "I enjoyed tonight. Thank you for the delightful dinner, and tomorrow is a good plan."

I entered the house.

As he walked to his car, he asked, "Same time good?"

"It is." Slamming the door, I stared at it while the evening's events raced through my mind.

"I recognized the slam," Janene said, startling me.

The two of them were seated in the living room. I dropped my keys inside my purse, placed it on the table by the door and dropped beside Rosa Leigh on the sofa.

"I thought males grew less complicated as they age," I said and sighed.

She patted my face. "None I've met do. How complicated are the men in your age group, Janene?"

"I'm a terrible judge of male character. I found my fiancé in bed with another woman the week before my wedding." She stood and shoved her feet into her house slippers. "I believe you can use a cup of herbal tea while you tell us about the evening. Do you want one, Rosa Leigh? I'm having one. Ives swears it's the cure for what ails you."

"It's good for sleep, not men trouble," I quipped.

Janene rushed into the kitchen. "Don't say a word until I return."

As we waited, the air conditioner whistled through the vent. The humming of the microwave and the clinking of a spoon against the cups broke the silence.

I walked into the kitchen. "I'll help carry the tea. You only have two hands."

While the other two sipped tea, I said, "The evening was wonderful. I felt the same chemistry between the two of us as when we were in high school. He acted like he felt it, too. But when we got back here, nothing. Not even a peck on the cheek." I covered my face with my hands. "And I wasted a breath mint I snuck into my mouth as we parked."

They laughed.

"Darn the man for being so inconsiderate to waste your breath mint," Rose Leigh said and kept on laughing.

"This isn't funny," I said. "He stirs up a lot of feelings I haven't felt in a long time and then dashes cold water on them."

"I think he's afraid to stir up his own feelings," Rosa Leigh said. "When he returned from college, he waited for you. Instead, you got married. He didn't date for several years after you married."

"He has no one to blame but himself. I asked him to come with me. He chose to stay here. I told him I was never coming back here to live," I said, the old hurt of his choice still there.

"And he told you," Rosa Leigh said, her voice stern, "all the time you were dating him, he didn't want to live anywhere else. You said when the time came, the two of you would work it out. And now you've returned to solve a case. You've made your home in Florida. Why would he want to open himself up to the pain again?"

For an instant, I stared daggers through her. "It sounds like you want to snatch him up for yourself."

She huffed. "You know better. We're as different as winter and summer, but I do love him like a brother. He's been there for me through divorces, my husband's sickness and death. Nothing would please me anymore than to see you two together again, but I know he'd be miserable doing what you want, and I know how determined you were about not moving back here. I'm asking you," she said and paused, her voice softening, "to tread cautiously and think about his feelings this time."

I stiffened. "Rosa Leigh you talk like I didn't consider his feelings last time. You remember the hours you and I spent discussing the two of us? You know I loved him, but he was stubborn and wouldn't leave here."

She smiled. "And you were stubborn and wouldn't stay. I haven't seen those traits improve in you over the years."

I looked at Janene. "You been around me for a while. Tell her I've changed."

Janene collected the two cups. "I've been silent while the two of you discussed this, but I'll answer your question with some of my own questions. Did you listen when you were asked not to search for the skull? Did you spend time in jail because you didn't do as the Sheriff asked? Did you follow Blake to the cave when he ordered you not to?" She disappeared into the kitchen.

Rosa Leigh placed her arms around my shoulder. "For the record, I love those traits in you. They are what's gotten you where you are today. Jaden gave you the life you dreamed about, a family, a career, travel, and all far away from here. Blake's made the same kind of life here. He's respected in this community. He loves his job, and he wants to work until they make him retire. What do you want with the rest of your life?"

She kissed my cheek and rose from the sofa. "I want you to stay and help me through chemo and radiation, but if you want to go back, I'll understand. Good night."

Her slippers scuffed down the hall, and the lock on her door clicked.

So much for understanding friends.

Janene flitted out of the kitchen and crossed the dining room. "I hope the tea helps you sleep. Goodnight."

Mentioning the tea again, triggered a memory. "Wait. I almost forgot. I have something to show you."

I took the bundle from the closet. "Ms. Overstreet brought this here tonight. I meant to tell the two of you when I came home from dinner, and . . . well, I got side-tracked."

I unwrapped the skull.

Janene's eyes grew big.

She sat on the sofa. "Do you know who it belongs to?"

I told her the details of why it came up missing, the tests done in Columbus and the results.

"You can tell Rosa Leigh in the morning. We can wind things up here and be on a plane by tomorrow evening or the next morning. Gabrielle will be excited to have us back. She's been carrying the load by herself and having to turn down cases. And there's damage to the agency from the storm. I need to go back and make some executive decisions," Janene said, her brown eyes sparkling with excitement.

She said a second goodnight and disappeared down the hall.

I thought about Rosa Leigh's request to stay.

How can I leave when she needs me? Then again, she doesn't want me to hurt Blake, and I might if I stay. How do I handle my feelings about him?

Chapter 31

After a night of tossing and turning, I woke with the same questions I went to bed with.

As usual, I rose earlier than the other two, and Simon greeted me as I passed Rosa Leigh's bedroom. He followed me to the kitchen.

I made my coffee and gave him a treat to hold him until after our walk. He gobbled the food and laid down by the door. I climbed onto a bar stool and drank my coffee.

I was rinsing my cup when a door down the hall opened. Simon and I sneaked out. The last thing I wanted was to resume last night's conversation.

I didn't notice sights, sounds or smells as I trailed behind Simon. He seemed to feel the jangle of nerves I was in and stayed close. When we reached the pond, he didn't offer to go in.

"Come on, Boy. Let's go back. I can't put this off any longer."

When the two of us entered the kitchen, Rosa Leigh said, "Good morning! Where have you been?" She was perched on a bar stool having coffee.

Simon put his head against her leg. She took it in both hands and kissed him.

I leaned both arms on the island. "You've never been an animal lover. Why did you buy him?"

She fluffed the fur on his head. "I didn't buy him. When he was a puppy, someone dropped him off on the side of the road, and I found him lying there, waiting for them to return. I knew if I left him, he would be killed. I looked for a home for him, but there were no suitable takers. And I grew to love him."

I thought about the changes my friend had gone through in her life. She wanted out of this town more than I, but she returned. She wanted money, clothes and a lavish lifestyle, and she married a little more money with each husband. I thought she'd married the last one only for his wealth, until I saw how devastated she was when he died. And because she loved him, she let him bring her back to the place she detested the most when we were young.

She looked at me. "I'm sorry about being so blunt last night, Ives. I didn't mean to hurt your feelings. Still, you need to know how broken Blake was when you—"

"Rosa Leigh, did she tell you the wonderful news?" Janene asked, bursting into the room.

A confused look spread over Rosa Leigh's face. She shrugged. "No."

I intended to share the news and the object myself, but Janene blurted the whole story. I wanted to bash her over the head with something. Instead, I rushed to the closet, unwrapped the skull and held it out, like Simon bringing us a find.

I felt the way Simon looks, too. I wanted Rosa Leigh's approval.

Janene's face reddened, and she lowered her head. "Sorry, Ives, not my story to tell."

Rosa Leigh looked up, her eyes questioning me before she said another word. "Does this mean you'll leave?"

Janene babbled on as she always does to try to smooth things over, "We can't stay. I packed before I went to bed last night. I'm certain we can purchase a ticket for tomorrow." She glanced at me and hitched her head toward the hall. "I'll leave you to your morning coffee."

"You're going?" Rosa Leigh asked.

The look of desperation on her face broke my heart.

"The last thing I want to do is leave you," I said and held her hands. "But if I stay and hurt Blake down the road, you'll never forgive me."

Water welled in her eyes, broke free and flowed down her cheeks. She sobbed uncontrollably. "What am I going to do? Who will drive me to treatments? Who's going to be here at night when I'm sick?"

I hugged her tight, and all was clear to me. She could hire someone to drive her to the treatments and to stay at night. What she couldn't buy was a friend to hold and comfort her like I could.

In that instant, I knew I couldn't leave.

"Let's talk," I said.

She raised her head off my shoulder, and I handed her a napkin. After she wiped her face, she yanked another napkin from the holder. As she slid off the stool, she picked up her coffee, led me into the living room and sat.

"Talk," she said.

"I can't leave you alone," I told her. "I'm having dinner with Blake tonight. I'll tell him your fears and explain why we can't see each other." I smacked my leg. "Heck fire, I'm too old to be dating an old sweetheart anyway."

She smiled and dabbed at a stray tear. "I didn't sleep much last night, but I did a lot of thinking." She blew out a long breath. "Not about you and Blake. About me. My breasts are a third of what makes me feminine. I'll lose my hair when I begin chemo." She heaved a breath and continued, "It will grow back, but for a while, I need someone to drag me into my new normal. I talked a positive talk about getting on with my life before, but the truth is, I lost my breasts, and I don't want to go out now. What will it be like when I have no hair, no eyebrows or lashes? Can you imagine how I'm going to look?"

"Stop the negative talk, Rosa Leigh. We'll prepare before it happens. We'll go shopping and buy you the sexiest wig on the market, and I'll take you to the 'Look Good, Feel Better' classes the American Cancer Center offers to learn how to do your makeup and wear your scarves. And, I'll take you today to buy a sports bra. They'll give you a shape, more than a lot of women with breasts. You've always been the most strikingly beautiful woman to walk into a room. You won't lose that."

She swiped her finger down my nose. "There's my friend. I thought I'd lost the one person who's always been able to encourage and inspire me to take another step when I thought I couldn't. I don't want to stand in the way of your chance for happiness, nor Blake's. You journey down the path as far as it takes you, but I hope you two marry."

I leaned forward and hugged her again. "I'll test the water tonight. Now, I'm going to tell Janene she will run the agency shorthanded, indefinitely. She may want to replace me or try to."

It doesn't take long to tell Janene my decision.

"I expected you to stay. Gabrielle and I will have to manage, and you'll still be a partner. We can discuss decisions over the phone."

Rubbing my hands together, I asked, "You mean I finally made partner in the JIG's Up Private Eye Agency?"

Janene tilted her head and said, "You've been a partner since you pestered us on the first case, my friend." She hugged me tight. "I'm going to miss you."

I hurried out of her room because I didn't want her to see the tears spilling down my cheeks. As I ran down the hall, my cell rang.

"I'm going to be late," Blake said. "It will be closer to eight before I arrive. Dress comfortably, though, because I have a surprise." Static crackled in the background, then voices. "Duty calls. See you."

CLICK.

I was wondering what the surprise could be when Janene appeared, her luggage clacking behind. "I caught a direct flight into Sarasota, and Gabrielle will pick me up. Will you take me to the local airport?"

Surprised, I asked, "What will we do with the rental?"

"I'm assuming Rosa Leigh will let you keep driving it. She rented it for us."

Rosa Leigh came out of her room, rubbing her wet hair with a towel. "I'd like you to drive it back to the airport and turn it in at the rental agency, Janene. Ives can drive my car anytime she needs it." She looked at me for approval.

I gave it to her with a slight nod.

Janene strolled to the front door. "Goodness, what a day!"

I tagged along behind her. When she turned, I hugged her. "Did you finish the novel?"

She did a little dance with her feet. "I completed the first draft." She hugged Rosa Leigh. "I cannot thank you enough for your hospitality."

Rosa Leigh chuckled and said, "Tell me the first book off the press is mine?"

"It is," Janene said and giggled. "Goodbye, my friend." As she walked out the door, she called back to us, "I'll miss you both."

"I'll miss you, too," I said and turned to Rosa Leigh. "I thought we could go shopping for your sports bra and wig."

"Not today."

"What am I going to do until Blake comes to get me?"

"Whatever you choose. I am going to do my hair," she said, leaving me alone with my thoughts.

Wandering into the kitchen, I did what I always do when I'm trying to solve problems. I baked.

By the time Blake arrived, I had all his favorite desserts: coconut pie, oatmeal raisin cookies and brownies.

When the doorbell chimed, I waved at Rosa Leigh. "Wish me luck."

She mouthed the words to me and smiled.

Outside, Blake took the box I was carrying and sniffed. "Is this what I think it is?"

"Your favorite desserts."

He placed the box on the back seat next to a picnic basket and slid beneath the wheel. "Remember our favorite spot?"

Smiling, I said, "On top of Copperhead Mountain."

He looked in his sidemirrors, backed out onto the road and drove up the hollow. "You know I've never been good expressing my feelings, but you and I loved each other once."

I opened my mouth to interrupt, but he raised his hand to stop me.

"We've both buried mates and went on as best we could. I still feel the same spark between us. I know you do. I wasn't certain I wanted to go through the hurt I felt before, until I thought about life without you again. I'm asking you to stay here long enough to see if we can rekindle the fire we once had. You don't have to tell me now," he said and chuckled. "But you're not coming off the mountain until you say you will."

"I told Rosa Leigh I'd stay and see her through her treatment, and it will take a year. Will twelve months be long enough?"

He pulled to the side of the road, leaned towards me, and I stretched across the middle thing-a-ma-gig.

I think my toes curled when his warm lips touched mine.

"Oh yes," I whispered. "The chemistry is still there, isn't it, but these new, fangled-dangled seat dividers are like my dad's flicking porch light telling me it's time to come inside."

Blake laughed and returned to driving.

"I'll steer cases to you that I think you might like, if you want to continue to be a private eye. And I know you never wanted to stay here, but there are snowbirds living here during the summer who winter in Florida or Arizona. We can work something out like that, if we want to continue our relationship. And I know Rosa Leigh would love to have you back. She can keep you busy with volunteer work—"

I placed my hand over his mouth. "I'm staying a year, Blake. Three hundred and sixty-five days will give us time to work out any problem."

"Or...I'll help you buy a building, and you can start a bakery. You can make good money baking for Nettie's restaurant."

I punched his shoulder. "Are you going to be this chatty all night?"

He grinned. "Only when I don't have food in my mouth, or when I'm not kissing you. We have lots of possibilities for the future, Ives. I might like to spend time in Florida. I've never been there. I'll consider becoming a snowbird."

I took his hand and kissed it. "We're grown-ups now. You're willing to compromise with me. And guess what? I've loved being here these last few weeks. It's been many years since I've spent a winter in Kentucky, but I'm staying with Rosa Leigh for a year to see her through her treatment. So, we will have enough time to woo each other and to see if the chemistry is there. And I think I can find enough private eye business to drive you crazy trying to keep me out of trouble."

I giggled and said. "I'm not as headstrong as I once was, Blake Sheets. Right this moment, I'm willing to go to the ends of the Earth, if you ask me."

Silence filled the car.

We were both content right where we were.

THE END

Acknowledgements

I wish to thank God who gives me the desire and talent to write, and my wonderful husband and family who believe in and support my journey.

I also want to thank Jo Ann Glim, author/photographer, who mentors and encourages me on a weekly basis, my fantastic editor, Sue Hallam, who has the patience of Job, my weekly critique group, The Uptown Writers of Bradenton, D. D. Scott of LetLoveGlow Author Services for her hard work, and all you fabulous readers who buy my books.

A special thank you goes to Pvt. Stephen Reddecker, who took a hike one Sunday afternoon and took a photo of the cave that had the jar, the walking sticks, the pole with a tattered remnant, and something white that looked like a skull, and to Roger Bloomfield and Vicki Barker who sent the photo to me. These people were the ones who planted the seed for Skull-Dug-Gery on Copperhead Mountain.

About the Author

Faye Henderson is a former middle school teacher with a Bachelor of Arts and a Masters' degree in early childhood education. She is the author of the JIGS UP Private Eye Series. The winner of numerous non-fiction and short story contests, her works have appeared in magazines, newspapers and anthologies. She is a member of Uptown Writers, SCBWI, FWA and FAPA organizations.

When she is not writing, Faye loves spending time with family and friends, walking nature trails, strolling the beach or painting. She resides with her husband in Florida during the winter and spends summers in Ohio.

Books by Faye Henderson

Jigs Up Mysteries:

Abandoned in the Everglades

Skull-Dug-gery on Copperhead Mountain

More Coming Soon!